One Fine Day

THE BAYSIDE BRIDES OF OYSTER BAY

OLIVIA MILES

ROSEWOOD PRESS

978-0999528471

One Fine Day

Copyright © 2019 Megan Leavell

Also by Olivia Miles

The Briar Creek Series

Mistletoe on Main Street

A Match Made on Main Street

Hope Springs on Main Street

Love Blooms on Main Street

Christmas Comes to Main Street

Harlequin Special Edition

'Twas the Week Before Christmas

Recipe for Romance

One

Sarah Preston stared at her phone in disbelief. Canceled! Her date for tonight had *canceled*. At eight thirty in the morning! As if suddenly, halfway through his second cup of coffee, he decided that he'd rather do something else with his evening. Something better.

And, as if that wasn't bad enough, he hadn't even rescheduled. Hadn't said much of anything really. *Sorry, but I can't make it tonight after all.* That was it. Hadn't even apologized. And boy, did he have an apology to make, not just for cancelling at the final hour, but for the new dress that hung from a hook on her closet door, and the new shoes to match, and the manicure that she had gotten last night after work. The one that was already chipped because in her fury she had reverted back to biting her thumb, the way she used to do back in school, when she was feeling particularly worked up about something like the Sadie Hawkins dance or term exams.

Between all of these items, half her weekly paycheck was gone. For nothing!

She stared at the brief message, even though she had it memorized, her mind trying to push back the excuses as quickly as they formed; after all, why should she be making up excuses for a man who hadn't even bothered to offer up one to her?

A man she hadn't even met. That was the worst of it. He hadn't even given her a chance.

She flopped back onto her unmade bed and stared at the overhead fan that was on overdrive. The weather was warming up, and the rain that had made the flower beds soggy and everyone's spirits damp all week had finally stopped. Sunlight poured in from the windows, showing promise of a beautiful weekend, the kind she usually looked forward to in Oyster Bay. Tourists had been flocking to town since Memorial Day weekend, and Main Street was bustling. She'd planned to wear those navy strappy sandals tonight with a bright pink handbag that would look adorable against that chambray sundress. She'd planned to tuck a pink cardigan of a similar shade into her bag in case the ocean breeze made her chilly come sundown. She'd planned to wear her hair up, off her neck, in case they sat outside and the humidity lasted into the evening instead. She had covered all her bases. Except for the part about him canceling.

She'd planned a lot of things. Too many. If she was being honest with herself, she shouldn't have even flirted with the notion that if things went well tonight, she might be able to casually invite her date to her friend Hannah's wedding in three weeks.

Now, she would be going to the event alone. As usual.

Sarah didn't know which was worse, frankly, that her date had canceled on her without even giving her a chance, or that she would have to go to Hannah's wedding alone, when she'd dared to think that this time, she wouldn't be stuck at the singles table with her boss Chloe. Once, there was a time when she held out hope that there might be an eligible bachelor at the singles table, but this was Oyster Bay, everyone knew everyone, and there were very few surprises. Besides, Hannah was marrying a local: Dan Fletcher. There wasn't even the hope of an out-of-town guest.

Sarah finally stood up after five more minutes of self-pity, straightened her skirt, inspected her chipped manicure, and decided that it was time to get to work. It was time for a lot of things, actually, but online dating was not one of them. Nope. Not for her. She'd forced herself to do it, for a thirty-day trial run, and the hope that had swelled within her the day she uploaded her profile was now almost tragic, really. She had even asked Hannah, who was a professional photographer, to take some photos of her down at the beach, and they had turned out lovely, truly, not only because of Hannah's artistic eye, but because Sarah had actually paid money to have her hair cut, layered, and blown out at the salon beforehand. Plus a "free" makeover where she got roped into buying a lipstick that was quite flattering, at least.

She'd put her best self out there. Written a peppy, breezy bio that she'd asked Hannah's sister Evie, a therapist and advice columnist, to review, as well as Abby, who was her closest friend in town and who possessed the kind of easy confidence that Sarah could only someday hope to have. Abby had suggested that she scale her bio way down, and Evie had agreed that the eight-hundred-word count was too much. And Melanie, another friend, even if she was her other boss, had suggested she refrain from mentioning that she worked at a bridal salon, just in case it sent the wrong sort of message. "Toss it in casually. On the first date," she'd suggested instead.

But now there would be no first date. Or a second date. Or date to Hannah's wedding. All that she had gotten out of her investment (well, emotional investment, because surely that had to count for something) was a canceled date with a guy named Rick from Shelter Port—three towns over.

Was Rick even his name? She narrowed her eyes on this thought as she pounded down the steps of her apartment building. And did he even own that golden retriever featured in all his photos, or had he borrowed it, to appeal to women who fell for that sort of thing? Women, admittedly, like her. After all, she thought, as she rounded the corner onto Main Street, who canceled a date that they had made, right down to a reservation at the fondue restaurant (how romantic was that?) without any excuse or suggestion of a rain check?

A man with a secret, that's who.

Or maybe, she thought, as she came to a stop outside

of Bayside Brides and took a long sigh as she looked at the beautiful display of summer gowns in the window, the strapless tulle ballgown being her current favorite, a man who just wasn't interested in finding the one, settling down, and living happily ever after.

Either way she saw it, it was a man who didn't care that he would never meet her. For all he knew she was his soul mate. The one.

She snorted. There was no such thing as the one. At least, not for her.

"It's official!" she announced as she pulled open the door to Bayside Brides and stepped inside the shop, sending off the wedding bells that hung from the hinge by a blue ribbon. The closest to the real thing she would ever get at this rate. "There's no such thing as a happily ever after. It's all a fairy tale! Sure, things start out all sweet and promising and full of hope, and then—"

From the counter, Melanie Dillon froze in alarm, and it was only then that Sarah noticed the woman being fitted into an ivory lace gown near the mirrors. Chloe Larson, co-owner of the shop along with Melanie, stared at Sarah in icy silence, her expression never losing its professional calm, before saying, "We had an early appointment today, Sarah. Mind grabbing our newest order of veils from the back room once you're settled in?"

Well, now she had done it. Sarah opened her mouth to apologize but she knew that now wasn't the time, not with the bride staring at her in a mix of both horror and, dare she say it, pity. From the steely look in Chloe's eyes, there might never be a time. It could just be that she lost more than her belief in finding love today. She may have just lost her job, too.

She swallowed hard as she beelined for the storage room, but she managed to catch Melanie's worried glance before she made it through the door.

She hadn't even hung her handbag on the coat rack before Melanie appeared. "What happened? I thought you had a date tonight!" she hissed.

"*Had* being the operative word." Sarah gave her a long look. As much as she appreciated the sympathy in her friend's expression, she also hated the way it made her feel as if she might cry. And she couldn't cry. Not when Chloe was fuming mad at her. And oh, that made her want to cry more than ever. "He canceled," she said, tossing up her hands.

"Well, maybe he got sick," Melanie said, but Sarah just shook her head as she searched the new boxes that had arrived yesterday for the veils that Chloe wanted.

"He didn't even bother to use that excuse. Besides, it's July. Who gets sick in July?" She pulled her phone from her bag and pulled up his text. She held out the screen to Melanie.

Melanie frowned. "Maybe something came up?"

"Maybe he went on another date, last night, and they hit it off. Or maybe he was never really interested in the date at all and decided to spare me. But the thing is that I was looking forward to it." Sarah leaned against a file cabinet. "I really thought this one might work out!"

"What were your interactions like?" Melanie asked. She slid the box containing the veils across the worktable and carefully cut through the seal with a pair of scissors they kept on hand for Melanie's custom wedding gown orders.

"You mean, our messages?" Sarah hesitated. "There weren't many, just a few getting-to-know-you type of exchanges. He likes to play tennis. And he's a dentist. And he has a dog." *Or so he said*. She chewed on her thumbnail and then, remembering her manicure, quickly dropped her hand again. "Do you think Chloe's mad at me?"

Melanie winced as she returned the scissors to the drawer. They were all paranoid about leaving sharps out with so many irreplaceable gowns at stake. "Do you want the truth or do you want me to make you feel better?"

Sarah groaned as she put her face in her hands. "Is it that bad?"

"Well, there was a client present—"

"But I didn't know there would be a client!" Sarah protested. "We never have clients this early." Usually, they didn't book clients until midmorning, once they all had a chance to settle in, check on their orders, and, of late, tend to the other services that the shop was now offering, including wedding consulting and custom gown design.

Melanie grimaced. "Just bring out the veils, act like nothing happened, and don't mention it again."

"And maybe Chloe won't either?" Sarah asked hopefully, but the look on Melanie's face confirmed her worst fears. Chloe was Melanie's cousin. She knew her well.

"I'll walk out with you and stand by the shoes, if it helps," Melanie offered.

"Thank you," Sarah gushed.

Of the two owners of Bayside Brides, Chloe was by far the more difficult to please. She was anxious, even uptight, but Sarah also knew that the store wouldn't be the success that it was without her high expectations. She had an eye for detail, and she was a perfectionist. When Sarah had joined the business in the winter and talk of expanding from a retail store to a full-service wedding business was being passed around, she'd dreamed of becoming a planner one day. Chloe was covering that for now, but she'd promised to let Sarah work with her on a fall wedding. Now Sarah wondered if she would keep to her promise.

With a shaky sigh, she grabbed the box of veils and squared her shoulders. She followed Melanie into the storefront, grateful that her friend was there for moral comfort, and hoping that she might be able to success-fully smooth things over with her cousin. The two often butted heads, but ultimately they had run a successful business together for years and had recently made moves toward expanding their services. Now wouldn't be the time to fire an employee, surely?

Chloe didn't look at her as she approached. The client was wearing another dress now, this one was a frothy chiffon with floral embroidery. It was also one of the dresses that Sarah had taken a photo of when she'd first unboxed it. She took photos of all of her favorite dresses, just so she would be prepared when her day finally came.

Only it wasn't coming, was it? Her date had been

canceled, and there wasn't another on the horizon. The other two "matches" she had made on the site had never returned her messages. How was she expected to compete with the hundreds of women whose profiles and photos were just as appealing, if not more so, than her own?

She was only aware that she was frowning when she caught Chloe's sharp eye. Instantly, she righted herself, forced a smile, set the veils on top of the jewelry counter, and backed away, hoping that her service was completed and that Chloe wouldn't call her over for anything else.

"Sarah!"

Damn. She closed her eyes. Briefly. Then, because she had to, she mustered up all her strength into a smile. "Yes?" she said weakly.

"Ms. Merrik would like to try on the satin kitten heels in a size eight."

Ms. Merrik? But the Merrik wedding was the one that Sarah had been hoping to help plan. She opened her mouth, but no sound came out, and from the knowing look in Chloe's eye, it didn't matter.

There was nothing she could say now. She had said enough already.

The only perk to the day was that it was, indeed, Friday, and that even though her date had canceled on her tonight, Melanie had offered to take her out for drinks instead. Once, it had been their weekly tradition. Girls' night. That's what they'd called it. But then Melanie went and fell in love with her oldest friend Jason, and girls' nights were fewer and farther between.

Honestly, it was probably the better option. After all, wasn't it more fun to sit with one of her dearest friends, in the comfort of flip-flops instead of those new strappy sandals which would have inevitably given her blisters, without the pressure of having to make witty conversation or worry that she had spinach between her teeth?

Really. Who needed a date when you had girlfriends?

That pick-me-up only worked for about the first ten minutes. By the time Melanie started talking about her plans with Jason for the weekend, something that had to do with a casual dinner at the Clam Shack and a long, lazy evening on the beach, Sarah's spirits deflated like someone had untied the balloon that was keeping her afloat.

She scanned the patio of Coast, a new establishment in town that was part of the Main Street renovation. It was crowded, and it was their first time snagging a table since it opened two weeks ago. This was something to be happy about, surely, except that right now all Sarah could see was a mass of couples, even though half were probably middle-aged. Summer was here, and the men wore khaki shorts and suede sandals, seersucker shirts rolled to the elbow, or golf shirts. The women wore navy, white, and pink of all shades. Sundresses, tank tops, striped blouses. Each table contained a colorful mixed bouquet, no doubt provided by Posy down at Morning Glory, the flower shop that they recommended to all their brides. There was a smell of salt in the breeze, and the sun was low in the peach-colored sky, and really, there should be a lot to look forward to right about now. Usually, summertime meant an influx of fresh faces. Last year this had perked her up. Now, little could lift her spirits.

She sank her straw deeper into her sangria and tried to stab a piece of diced fruit. She had bigger problems at the moment than the sad state of her love life. "On a scale of one to ten, how much trouble do you think I'm in?"

Melanie looked like she was being strangled. She took another sip of her wine, nearly draining the glass.

"Ballpark estimate," Sarah said. She could take it. Now was the time to dish on all the pain at once. Tomorrow could only get better from here. "If you had to guess."

Melanie chewed her lip. "If I had to guess?" She blinked a few times. "Maybe...a nine?"

"Nine!" Sarah realized she had shouted this louder than she'd planned when she saw the people at a few other tables glance her way. She leaned across the table, lowering her voice to an urgent whisper. "*Nine?*"

"Well, what were you expecting me to say?" Melanie said, her eyes wide with apology.

"I don't know. A six? Seven, tops." Sarah leaned back in her chair, clutching her glass of sangria. Melanie was smart enough to flag down the waitress and signal for another round. "Nine? Really?"

Melanie reached for her glass and then realized it was empty. "Maybe she'll forget about it by tomorrow."

They exchanged a look. Sarah speared a slice of apple. Hard. Both knew that this was wishful thinking. Bayside

Brides catered to brides, fed into the fairytale of the picture-perfect, magical wedding day. And Sarah had just announced that she didn't believe in any of that. Some brides were twitchy, already nervous, and doubting their choices (and not just which shoes they had selected). Sarah had punctured the fantasy.

"Are you really giving up on love just because one guy canceled?" Melanie asked. "For all you know, he could be a serial killer. Maybe he spared you."

"A serial killer?" Sarah snorted. Sadly it would almost be better to have been spared than rejected.

"I never liked the idea of you meeting up with a stranger," Melanie said, and now it was Sarah's turn to look at her as if she were crazy.

"But you were the one who talked me into trying online dating again!" she cried. She'd done it before, years ago. One guy had spent the entire date talking about his ex-girlfriend. The other had just been released from jail for a white-collar crime. She should have known better.

"Was I?" Melanie's brow knitted. She smiled up at the waitress who cleared their empty glasses and set the fresh drinks on the table. "All I know is that you, me, and Jason made a pact this spring. This year would be different. Better. This is our time to reach for what we want."

"And you and Jason figured all that out rather quickly," Sarah said, reaching in for her glass. It was easy for Melanie to say. She and Jason had been best friends forever. They only had to finally open their eyes to realize that they were destined to be more than that. So now they were a couple, no doubt they'd be getting married eventually too, and Sarah... "I don't have any guys in my life to start dating. Anyone I meet will be a stranger."

"It's summer," Melanie pointed out. "Tourist season."

Last summer this had cheered her. Not so anymore. "And date a guy who will be going back to New York or Boston or wherever come August? No thanks."

"Tell you what, I'll have a long chat with Chloe and smooth things over if you give the very next man that you meet a fair chance, even if the circumstances don't seem perfect," Melanie said.

"Doesn't that fall under the category of blackmail?"

"It's a friend wanting to see you happy."

Technically, Melanie was her boss, but Sarah wasn't going to get into semantics right now. And she could use any help she could get when it came to getting back on Chloe's good graces.

Sarah stared at her friend. "What if he's eighty? Or sixteen? Or...Tim?"

Melanie laughed. "I mean the first eligible man. Age appropriate. Not Tim Wright."

"Poor Tim," they both said in unison, and then Sarah did laugh, a good hard laugh that she hadn't felt all day and deeply needed.

"Do you think Tim will ever get married?" Sarah asked, thinking of the poor guy whose mother desperately tried to pawn him off on every single girl in town, once giving him such a strong shove of encouragement that he nearly lost his footing.

"There's someone for everyone if you ask me," Melanie said.

Someone for everyone. Once, Sarah had believed that. A part of her possibly still did. But the logistics of finding that person in this great, big, wide world felt as impossible as finding that person in this tiny little town of Oyster Bay.

"I guess Tim's always a fallback option," she said mournfully, but the truth was that she would rather be single than with the wrong man, even if Tim's last name was Wright, a pun that his overbearing mother loved to remind every single woman in Oyster Bay, often with a larger than life wink and a chuckle that ended with a snort.

"You have to keep an open mind," Melanie said. "I know you. You go for the same type of guy every time. Good looking. Outgoing. No real interest in long-term commitment."

Sarah pursed her lips. Melanie was right about all that.

"I used to go for the same type too. If I'd kept that up, I would have ruined my chance with Jason."

This too was true. Melanie was all about the jocks and players before. And Jason. Well, Jason was marriage material. Jason was courteous, polite, reserved, sweet, and kind. He wasn't thrilling. He wasn't unexpected. He wasn't going to send Melanie on the emotional roller-coasters that she had become addicted to over time.

Maybe, just maybe, Melanie had a point.

"Fine," Sarah said, hoping she wouldn't live to regret

this. "The very next eligible man that I meet, I will give him a fair chance."

Melanie grinned with satisfaction. "I can't wait to see what happens."

Sarah picked up her drink. Normally, she'd say the same, but that was a dangerous way of thinking, and from here on out, she was playing it safe.

Two

Chris Foster pulled his car to a stop at the base of the long, gravel drive and frowned. He'd gotten an early start, mostly because he'd been unable to sleep last night, and it wasn't even midmorning when he'd crossed the town line into Oyster Bay, his summer destination for most of his childhood, and often some years after that. Check-in at the hotel wasn't until noon. He didn't feel like hanging out on Main Street. The beach no longer held the appeal it once did. There was no avoiding what he'd come here to do.

With a sigh, he pushed his foot down on the accelerator and forced the vehicle to the end of the drive where it met the garage, or carriage house, he supposed it was called. Above the four garage spots, the attic held nothing but garden equipment and dust bunnies, of this he was sure after many rainy, humid afternoons of his boyhood spent playing up there, usually by himself or with Uncle Marty's sweet old Lab, Russ.

What he was not so sure of was the condition of the main house itself. His uncle hadn't lived here in nearly as long as Chris had been back—three years. Even then, the house was showing signs of neglect: shingles were missing from the roof, paint on the window trim was cracked and peeling, and the furnace seemed to be working overtime to keep up with these Maine winters. By then, his uncle was down to just a housekeeper and a gardener who only visited three seasons of the year, and Janice, the housekeeper, was getting on in years, just like him. More than anything, Chris had come to realize that Janice was Marty's companion. He was lonely. Widowed before he had fathered any children. Chris's visits were the highlight of his year, he used to say.

Chris didn't even realize he was clenching his teeth until his jaw began to ache.

He pulled to a stop near the rose trellis, surprised to see that the flowers had at least been pruned, and that perhaps some maintenance had continued over the years. Who had set this up, he couldn't be sure. The house had belonged to his grandparents, and when they passed, Marty took over. It was of no interest to Chris's father, who preferred Boston, and his more reasonably sized home in Cambridge. His father wanted to sell this place off to a developer—something he and Marty had argued over when their parents passed, and eventually Marty had bought him out. Chris supposed it was fortunate that history wouldn't repeat itself. He was an only child, himself. Had no brother to squabble with over the inheritance of this big, old, seaside mansion. He could do with it as he pleased.

He climbed out of his SUV and closed the door firmly behind him, shoving the keys into the pocket of his jeans. His hands touched something metal there, another key, the one to this house, the one Marty's attorney back in Boston had slid across the desk to him last week when Marty's last will and testament were read to his remaining relatives. Chris had inherited the property, which came as only a mild surprise but still felt strangely surreal. His housekeeper and companion, Janice, had received a generous lump sum. Much of the liquid assets had gone to various charities.

Personally, he'd been hoping for a watch—the gold one that Marty always had on his wrist. He'd been hoping that all this was a bad dream, really. There'd been enough loss of late.

He forced himself to walk over the gravel, the salty sea breeze filling his lungs. It was a beautiful day, a day not so different than the ones he used to spend here as a boy each summer. A day not so different from the day he'd married Jenna, right out back, on the huge terrace facing the elaborate garden.

One foot in front of the other. Keep moving forward. He'd gotten good at that over the years. Mastered it. But being back here...He was stumbling.

He had parked near the back of the house, and it would be a long walk to the front, but that wasn't why he went through the kitchen entrance, not really. It was out of habit. Out of some memory that was ingrained in him, even if he wanted to banish it. Days filled with running through the gardens that stretched all the way to the Atlantic, standing with his bare feet in the sand, letting the waves crash at his legs, not caring if his clothes got wet, and not going back inside until the last bit of light had started to fade.

Chris tried the door first, for some reason surprised that it was locked, and then saddened by this discovery, this hard, cold evidence that things had changed and that they could never again be what they were. They'd hit him in waves, recently. Somehow it was easier thinking of Marty, here in the house, a vague promise to someday return, even if he knew deep down that it might never happen.

Now, it couldn't happen. Marty was gone. And he'd never even said good-bye.

With a tight jaw, Chris fished out the key, stuck it in the lock, and turned. It didn't go easily, but eventually, he heard the lock click and the door pushed open, swelling against the doorjamb. It was stifling inside the house. Marty never had gotten around to installing central air. Said he preferred to keep the windows open anyway, to let the breeze blow in off the Atlantic, especially in the evenings.

Now, Chris walked to the closest window, just above the sink. He grunted at the force—the wood had expanded and he barely wedged it free. Old windows. Old house. The floorboards creaked under his weight.

He stared out the window, onto the terrace, feeling the fresh air on his face, and he could almost feel the presence of all the others, the ghosts of moments past, the sound of the band, the smell of the food, the touch of her hand.

He trained his eyes on the ocean, at the waves that pushed and pulled against the shore. At some point, he would turn around, take in this house, and force himself to have one last good look at it.

And then, he would sell it. And maybe then, he would finally be free.

Sarah usually made every effort to be early, or at least on time, to work, especially on the occasional weekends when Melanie had the day off from the shop to work on custom dress orders and it would just be her and Chloe manning the storefront. Those days were busy and stressful, and Sarah was always sure to be dressed in her finest, and careful to watch her every move. No receipts left out on the counter where other clients could see them. No shoes left out of their boxes where someone might trip. Phone calls to clients should be taken in the back room rather than upfront (things could get personal, and there were often tears, as it was amazing how much emotion could be brought out in the weeks leading up to the big day!). But today, knowing that she had no friend as a buffer and that on a scale of one to ten, Chloe was probably at about a twelve with her rather than a nine (Melanie was kind that way), Sarah waited in the window of Angie's until her watch struck the last minute before the shop opened for business.

Her stomach went all funny when she stood up and pushed in her chair.

"You feeling okay, Sarah?" Leah asked from behind the counter. A relative newcomer to the café, she was always happy to supply the women of Bayside Brides with treats throughout the day, considering they were regular customers. Sure enough, she reached into the glass display case and shoved something into a white paper bakery bag. "On the house. Chocolate cures everything, if you ask me."

Sarah managed a smile as she approached. "Thanks, Leah. Angie's lucky to have you."

"Don't I know it," Leah grinned, and Sarah's hand shook as she reached for the bag. Could her boss say the same about her?

Today's treat was a brownie, she could tell by the weight of it. She'd eat it on her lunch break. If she still had a job by then.

Oh, dear. There went that funny feeling in her stomach again.

Sarah hurried to the crosswalk and pressed the button, waiting for the signal, but her eyes kept darting to the shop, which looked so innocent from a distance, so sweet and inviting, with a white awning that rippled in the breeze and a glass-paned door painted in the store's signature shade of blue. The planters that flanked it were always filled with boxwoods, but around each Chloe tended to add some seasonal flowers for color—currently, they were pink pansies.

And there was Chloe now, in the window, turning the cute little oval-shaped vintage sign on the door. Damn it. Now Sarah was late. That would be two strikes against her in two days. She couldn't make it three. Three would definitely be grounds for termination, and then what? What would she do?

Her passion was all things weddings! It always had been! She'd been subscribing to bridal magazines forever. She loved the flowers and the dresses and the cakes and the rings. She loved the fantasy. The dream of one special day when you got to be a real live princess, or the closest thing to it. She positively longed to wear a tiara. And a ball gown. And a train.

But she'd given up on finding all that for herself. Could Chloe blame her? After all, Chloe was also unattached. Though, unlike Sarah, Chloe didn't seem bothered by this fact.

And really, Sarah shouldn't be so bothered by it either. She was single. By choice. She had given up! So she'd agreed to Melanie's challenge. It was a ridiculous one and also an opportunity to officially silence her suddenly optimistic friend once and for all. Melanie was dating the town doctor. He had adored her all his life. She'd found her happily ever after. It didn't mean everyone else would find it just as easily.

But...she had to check that attitude—and quick. Her stomach heaved as she pushed through the door, the wedding bells jangling her arrival. One scan of the room revealed an empty storefront, ready for the day to start. The jewelry case glistened nearly as much as the towering case of tiaras. The veils were fluffed and hanging from their vintage-style rack. The shoes were neatly organized against the far wall, by style, their boxes tucked underneath in various sizes. And the dresses...She would never tire of the dresses. Three walls of wedding gowns in all styles. Bridesmaid and flower girl options were housed in the corner.

Chloe must be in the storage room, Sarah determined. Or the dress closet. Or organizing a dressing room. Sometimes, when there was time, Chloe would hand-select a few gowns in expectation of her client's arrival. She had exquisite taste and could tell what would look good on everyone's figures—sometimes it warded off unnecessary frustration when a bride wanted a gown that didn't best fit her shape.

But today there didn't appear to be any gowns hanging from the hooks near the dressing room doors.

With growing dread, Sarah pushed through the storage room door to see Chloe making an herbal tea with water from the electric kettle. No food or beverages were allowed in the storefront, and for good reason.

"Good morning!" Sarah smiled brightly, hoping her warm greeting would show that all had returned to normal. She was her cheerful, happy, loved all things romance self, and Chloe was...

Still an ice queen.

Chloe's smile was tight as she tapped her spoon against the rim of her mug—blue, to match the shop's color scheme, of course. Her equally blue eyes seemed to home in on Sarah, who turned her back to hang her tote bag on a hook. Normally she liked to settle into the day before the flurry of clients arrived, but today she willed for an early appointment, a walk-in, even a disgruntled mother-in-law, or a jealous maid of honor. They'd seen it all.

"It's nice that the rain from last week finally let up!" Sarah said in a shaky voice. Her tone was overly chipper, even to her own ears. She was being forced. She wondered if Chloe could see it too.

"Not soon enough." Chloe shook her head. "I just found out last night that the Hillside Winery flooded. Someone left a window open."

"Oh no!" The Hillside Winery was a popular wedding reception spot. The vineyard was small, but the house was set on a hill, with a beautiful view of the fields and vaulted ceilings in the reception hall that allowed for oversized chandeliers to hang dramatically. "Was there much damage?"

Chloe's eyes widened. "Extensive. And mold. They have to completely renovate the entire cellar."

Sarah frowned as she considered the implications. "But that's where Hannah is getting married."

"Make that where she *was* planning to get married," Chloe corrected. Hannah Donovan had been Chloe's first client when she branched her services into wedding planning this spring. Even though Hannah was a low-key bride and a friend to them all, Sarah also knew how much pride Chloe took in her services...and how fearful she had always been of anything going wrong. "Now we have to figure out a new plan."

"Does she have a back-up venue in mind?" Sarah asked, hating herself for being almost grateful that they were able to focus on this problem rather than her lack of professionalism yesterday.

"On this short of notice?"

Of course. The wedding was only weeks away. Three weeks from today, in fact.

"What about the Harper House Inn?" Sarah suggested, even though she was fairly sure that Chloe had already considered this, and that she would have considered anything that Sarah could even come up with. Still, it kept the conversation going, and she did want Hannah's wedding to be a success. She was marrying her high school sweetheart after they'd gone their separate ways years ago. If that didn't remind her that romance was still alive and blooming, she didn't know what would.

Well, it only bloomed for some, she thought.

Chloe set down her mug and walked back toward the door to the storefront. Seeing no other choice, Sarah followed her into the room on shaky knees. If only Melanie wasn't doing home visits for custom gowns today!

"The Harper House Inn is always a fallback," Chloe said.

"And Hannah has an emotional attachment to it," Sarah pointed out. She walked over to the oversized flower arrangement that they kept on a central table, hoping for something to do, but of course, it appeared that Chloe had already tended to fresh water. "Hannah practically grew up with her cousins in that house. And it's a beautiful location." An old Victorian mansion on the shore. Really, what more could anyone ask for?

"It is. But I think Hannah wanted something of her own. Margo and Bridget were both married there, after all." Chloe tossed up her hands. "I know her father would be happy to host it at The Lantern, but it's probably too casual, even for Hannah. I don't see many other options, though. The Oyster Bay Hotel is booked. So is the Botanic Garden. I'll see about the library today. They have that room on the top floor with beautiful stained glass. It's my job to fix this mess."

"You can't help that her venue flooded," Sarah remarked. "It's not like she has a ripped seam and you can quickly stitch up the back of the dress. Besides, you've overseen every inch of this wedding." And it was true. Every element of this wedding was flawless, in a style perfectly befitting to the bride. In this case, it was light, airy, somewhat casual but still elegant. Chloe had nailed everything from the font on the invitations to the exact shade of teal blue ribbon that would be wrapped around the bouquets—a colorful mix of flowers that was both elegant and whimsical.

Chloe gave a little shrug, but it was clear that she wasn't convinced. She walked around the counter and stared at her appointment book, and even though Sarah knew that perhaps she was off the hook, that perhaps yesterday's disaster was replaced with today's, she didn't feel right just letting it hang there, never knowing when it would come up, or how long it might lurk.

"About yesterday," she blurted, now wishing she hadn't said anything at all when she saw Chloe's icy gaze cut across the room. She gripped her hands together until they hurt. "I want to apologize. I didn't know that a client would be here."

"We're open to the public," Chloe said. "You should always assume that a client will be here."

Sarah felt her shoulder sag. Leave it to Chloe to make this more difficult than it already was. "I feel terrible. I should have kept my personal problems to myself."

"Correct," Chloe said, letting her eyes drift back to the book. For a moment Sarah thought that the worst of it was over, that Chloe was going to drop it there. Instead, Chloe came around the side of the counter.

"And I didn't realize that was...the Merrik client." She held her breath, hoping that Chloe had cooled off, that maybe the bride had found it funny, maybe even flattering that she was amongst the lucky ones.

Chloe just raised an eyebrow. "I can't think about this right now with everything else I'm dealing with at the moment. We can discuss it on Monday. At the staff meeting."

Monday. It meant she still had a job. But it also meant she wasn't off the hook just yet.

She walked over to the flower girl dresses and began fluffing the skirts, even though they were already fluffed. Sweet little dresses. The pink one in front was the same style Hannah's two flower girls would wear.

"So, will you be at Hannah's bridal shower tonight?" Sarah asked, eager to make lighthearted conversation even though of course she wished the answer was that no, Chloe wouldn't be there to spoil the fun and stress her out and make her a nervous wreck the entire time.

"Evie and Kelly asked me to help plan it," Chloe replied.

Of course. "Well, I can cover the afternoon if you want to head out early to set up," Sarah offered. It would be chaotic, especially with Melanie out for the day, but she could manage. And maybe, just maybe, it would help her to earn her way back into Chloe's good graces.

Or at least buy her some much-needed space, she thought, breathing a sigh of relief when the first client of the day pushed into the shop, her eyes taking in the goods like a child would enter a candy shop.

She'd have to find a way to prove to Chloe that she was a good hire. Until then, distance was best, she thought, as she moved to the storage room to check on some orders that she had technically checked on yesterday.

Three

The real estate office was located in the heart of downtown Oyster Bay, and Chris had already set up the meeting earlier in the week, hours after he learned that he was now the sole owner of the property that was commonly known as Crestview. He arrived early, happy to relax in the comfort of the cool, temperature-controlled waiting room, next to an oversized, waxy plant and a stack of magazines, his back to the window with its view of Main Street.

"Chris?" A man a couple of years older than himself appeared in the entranceway near the front desk. "Jeff McDowell. Pleased to meet you."

"Thanks for meeting me on such short notice," Chris said, standing to shake his hand. Jeff looked vaguely familiar, and judging from the way that he was frowning, perhaps he felt the same.

"Come on back to my office," Jeff said, leading him down a short hallway to an office that held a desk and two grey upholstered visitor chairs. There was a framed photo on a file cabinet of two boys. His kids, no doubt. "So, you've inherited the Foster estate." He raised his eyebrows, seeming impressed, or perhaps he was just mirroring Chris's feelings. It was overwhelming. It was too much. It needed to go away.

"It belonged to my uncle, and my grandparents before that. I spent every summer there as a child."

"Ah." Jeff nodded, his grin one of satisfaction. "I thought you looked familiar."

"I didn't get to know any of the kids in town, but yeah, you probably saw me around." He cleared his throat. He didn't need to go down memory lane. "The place is too big for me, and my home is in Boston. I'd like to list the property."

With any luck, he could be out of here by tomorrow.

Jeff was still nodding, but now his smile had turned to something tenser. "I'm afraid that it won't be as straightforward as you might hope."

Chris frowned. "It's old and it needs some work, but it's oceanfront. Aren't people climbing over each other to find property like that?"

"Yes—"

"Or a developer," Chris said, but something in his stomach tightened at that thought. It was one thing to sell the house. It was another to know it would be torn down. He blinked, forcing back that ache in his chest that was creeping in. No, let it go. Let it go completely. It was better that way. After all, what was he supposed to do with it? "My father found an interested developer years ago. Surely that land is worth something."

"Technically, yes—"

"What do you mean, technically?" Chris could feel his blood pressure rising. It was bad enough that he'd have to pay property taxes on the place. Now he was being told there wasn't a market for it?

"Your uncle's house is now a registered historical landmark," Jeff explained.

Chris swore under his breath. "That sounds ominous."

"It means that selling to a developer is no longer an option. And unfortunately, the historical status, coupled with the condition of the home, may make it a tough sell, even with its prime location. Not every buyer wants a fixer-upper, and just from a glance at the property, it's obviously behind on routine maintenance. Of course, I haven't been inside yet." Jeff dared to look optimistic.

Chris shook his head. There was no need to hold out false hope here. He thought about the closet door handle that had come off in his hand. The wallpaper that was peeling. The paint that was flaking. And all that was from a cursory walk-through before coming here. There was no way the plumbing was up to code. He tossed up his hands. "So what are my options?"

Jeff shrugged. "We'll go over to the house after this so I can assess the value. We can put it on the market. You never know. The right buyer might walk in here tomorrow."

And good old Marty might walk right through that door, Chris thought miserably.

"You'll want to get it ready to list," Jeff advised. He slid a stack of papers across the desk to Chris. "This is a list of regulations for properties registered as a historical landmark. Any changes that exceed those permitted and stated here will have to be approved by the committee."

"Red tape," Chris muttered, pulling the stapled papers closer. He briefly leafed through them. "I don't have time for this." He had clients in Boston, clients who wanted his attention, who didn't want to hear that he wasn't in front of a computer screen, watching the markets, but instead, petitioning a small-town committee to allow him to replace a leaky faucet. Yes, the kitchen faucet was dripping, too.

Jeff frowned. "I'm afraid there aren't many options. Is the house still furnished?"

"It is," Chris said, pushing the list of rules and regulations away from him. From what he could tell, there was next to nothing he could do to the property to improve it or even bring it up to code. Even the shingles on the roof could only be replaced with ones of similar architecture. That house had a slate roof. He felt a headache coming on.

"I'd suggest an estate sale," Jeff said. "Normally I would stage an empty house, but given its age, I think in this case it will be better to show it as a blank canvas, or clear out some of the older items, give it a fresh feel. And you never know; an estate sale could drive traffic. A potential buyer could walk in and fall in love with the place."

Chris met Jeff's gaze. "Level with me, here. Am I going to be stuck with this property forever?"

"Not if I have anything to do with it. To open your options, I will list this as a commercial property as well as a residential home. This would make a fine artist retreat. Or a small hotel. You never know."

In other words, he was grasping at straws. Still, Chris appreciated it.

"I could recommend someone to oversee the estate sale," Jeff said. "Do you have to leave town soon?"

Technically, he did not. His job as a financial planner allowed him to work remotely, on his own schedule. "I appreciate that, but I feel like I owe it to Marty to go through his remaining things myself."

Jeff gave a small smile. "Of course. He was a fine man. Didn't know him well, but when he came into town he was always friendly. Philanthropic, too. He sponsored my sons' baseball teams one year."

Chris's brow knitted in confusion, but he was smiling. "Really? He always did like baseball." He'd given him a ball one year, signed by every player on the Red Sox. Chris still had it back at his condo, on a shelf in his living room. It was one of his most prized possessions and one of his only keepsakes from childhood, other than the postcards his parents mailed to the boarding school he attended. In the summers, it was his turn to send them postcards, which he picked up in town, right here on Main Street.

"He was a fine man," Jeff said again.

He was, Chris thought, pulling in a breath as he stood to leave. A fine man with a dilapidated mansion that Chris was now stuck with for the foreseeable future. Fortunately, he'd never been one to shy away from a challenge. Still, something told him that nothing about this was going to be as easy as he'd hoped.

At seven that night, armed with a set of champagne flutes boxed and wrapped in glittery white paper and tied with a gold ribbon, Sarah walked up the steps to the front porch of the Harper House Inn: a house that the Harper sisters had grown up in, now owned by Bridget, the eldest, who had transformed the property into a charming inn. Abby, the youngest, was the chef, there. Well, cook, technically, seeing as she'd learned all her skills at home rather than through formal training, but she was so good at what she did that she was a chef in all their eyes. What had started with breakfast had turned into afternoon weekend tea and soon dinner would be added a few nights a week.

Sarah knew that Abby had insisted on catering Hannah's wedding, and she and Chloe had had many meetings about the menu, going over it again and again, leaving Abby to sometimes widen her eyes across the shop at Sarah when Chloe was distracted by something in one of her many folders: budgets, schedules, paper and fabric samples. And menus, of course.

It will all be okay, she told herself as she reached the last step. So Chloe would be here tonight. But so would all her friends.

A middle-aged couple was sitting on the porch swing, fingers intertwined, and she gave them a polite smile, feeling as if she had interrupted a private moment, a romantic evening, a country weekend getaway, a little alone time after dinner. All things she would never know.

She checked that bout of self-pity at the door and let herself into the lobby, which was relatively quiet for a Saturday evening. One glance to the right showed an empty dining room, and another to the left marked a cozy lobby where a single guest sat in a leather armchair, reading near a crackling fire. Bridget liked to keep it going for ambiance, even though the evenings were growing warmer by the day.

She walked through the room to the sun porch at the back, which had been closed off for Hannah's party this evening. Still, Sarah couldn't help but wonder how this was supposed to work. They weren't the wildest group of women, but they weren't exactly all quiet when they got together, either.

But of course, Chloe had thought of a solution for this. In addition to the closed French doors, there were billowing sheets of fabric for privacy. Leave it to Chloe, Sarah thought ruefully. She may not be the easiest person to work for, but she was certainly impossible not to respect.

She opened the door to the porch, making sure it closed behind her, and gasped. What was a simple porch and an extension of the lobby in many ways had been transformed into a chic, airy, elegant party room, complete with fairy lights and candelabras that anchored a buffet table covered in a white tablecloth. Bunches of bright, colorful flowers accented the otherwise white space, and even the throw pillows that Bridget kept on the armchairs and settees had been replaced to fit the color scheme of sea foam blue and white.

"I seriously couldn't have pulled this together better myself," Margo hissed in Sarah's ear as she took the gift from her hand. "I mean, I was happy to do it, with Hannah being my cousin and all, but Evie and Kelly wanted to take over, as they should, with Chloe's help. I figured they were just trying to toss a little business over to you guys at Bayside Brides, but this." She shook her head as they both took in the room. Even the floorboards had been replaced by rugs that matched the flowers.

"Is that...blue punch?" Sarah marveled.

"Yep," Evie said, coming up beside them. "And there are even little umbrellas to drop onto the side of your glass. A different color for each guest so they don't get mixed up. I mean, Chloe thought of every detail."

"I'm definitely going to hire Chloe to do my wedding," Kelly said. "I mean, if I get married."

Which was a likely scenario, given how much her boyfriend Noah adored her.

Sarah couldn't help it. All at once, all she could think of was how amazing it would be to have a party like this for herself. To have a bridal shower, full of her closest friends, to have so much ahead of her to look forward to.

Instead, she'd have to settle for being a guest. And, seeing as she'd walked here from town to work off some of her anxiety, she was going to have a glass or two of that punch.

Hannah was helping herself to a glass, and Sarah leaned in to hug her. "Congratulations! Are you getting excited?"

Hannah blinked as if she were holding back tears. "I'd be more excited if my venue hadn't flooded."

Sarah set a hand on her arm. "You know it will be a beautiful day wherever it's held. Look at how Chloe transformed this space!"

"I know.'" Hannah looked down at her drink. "I always told myself I'd never be one of those brides, you know? But then I became a bride, and well..."

Sarah nodded. She understood.

"Dan says it doesn't matter where we get married. That he'd marry me at town hall. But I want it to be beautiful. I want photos." Hannah laughed. "I'm already turning into a pest with that, too, telling the photographer exactly which shots I want. I'd do it myself if I could."

Hannah was a talented photographer, but Sarah said, "You'll be too busy dancing with your new husband to even think about the photos."

"I hope you're right," Hannah said earnestly. She sighed, then looked around the room. "Well, I suppose I should greet my guests."

Sarah watched her go, hoping that some miracle

could happen and soon, and sighed as she reached for a glass.

"How was work today?" Melanie whispered, coming up beside her.

Sarah darted her eyes over her shoulder to where Chloe was sitting on a sofa talking with the guest of honor.

"The best I could hope for, I suppose," she said, turning back to reach for a glass. "How was your fitting with Samantha King?" She knew from several talks with Melanie that Samantha was turning into one of those special sorts of bridezillas that came along every once in a while. They came in different forms, of course. Some changed their orders a hundred times. Others didn't like anything. Others brought their bridesmaids to tears when they shoved ugly brown dresses onto them.

And then there were the clients who were never satisfied. Samantha was one of them.

"She decided to change the design again," Melanie said as they stood sipping their punch. The logical thing to do would be to cross the room and sit with the others, who were now slowly joining Chloe and Hannah on the wicker chairs and sofas, and they would, soon, but it seemed that Melanie was eager to have her story told out of earshot, and Sarah couldn't blame her. After all, Chloe hadn't been particularly enthusiastic about having Melanie make custom gowns. She was concerned about many scenarios, including this one.

Chloe would be asking if Melanie was charging Samantha for each redesign, Sarah knew, and she knew

Melanie well enough to know that she was too nice to bother with this, even if it probably was the professional thing to do at this point. Melanie wanted all her brides to be happy. She'd go to great lengths to ensure that.

They all would. That's why they were such a great team.

A funny feeling stirred in Sarah's stomach. "Well, I suppose we should join the others," she said, a little reluctantly. What she'd really like to do right about now was drink back the rest of her punch, slip out the back door, and go for a walk on the beach. Nothing soothed her soul more than the feeling of sand between her toes and the wind in her hair.

Instead, she moved to sit between two of the Harper sisters. Chloe was across the coffee table, and Melanie wedged in beside her on the small couch. For cousins, they couldn't look more different, Chloe with her long, silky, smooth blonde hair, and Melanie with her darker waves. But they both had small, upturned noses. Both had long legs that they crossed in the same direction, and hands that they folded on their kneecaps.

"When I was in town today, I ran into Jim. He said that Crestview Manor might be coming on the market," Bridget said, and, across the table, Hannah's eyes went round.

"I love that house! Oh my goodness, Evie, remember how we used to ride our bikes up to the gates and stare inside?"

"Do I!" Evie's mouth pinched as she squeezed into a seat between her two sisters and rearranged a throw pillow behind her back. "I can still remember the time you made me hoist you over the brick wall so you could take some photos of the flower garden. Then you couldn't get back over. I've never pedaled home so quickly in my life. Nearly lost my footing!"

Hannah laughed but brushed it away with a wave of her hand. "I just took the shoreline home. Came back for my bike the next day." She smiled wistfully. "I always thought that was the most interesting house in all of Oyster Bay."

"It sounds like it!" Their youngest sister Kelly, who had grown up with their mother on the West Coast, looked a little lost as she sipped her drink.

"I'll take you by it some time," Hannah promised, and Kelly beamed. "I always thought that would be the perfect place to get married. Right there in that colorful garden, with the sea in the distance and that giant stone house in the backdrop."

Sarah sat up a little straighter and skirted a glance in Chloe's direction. Was she catching this? She must be. Chloe didn't miss anything. She was sharp like that.

"But it's practically crumbling," Evie pointed out, ever the pragmatic one.

"But that's what makes it so charming!" Hannah insisted. She gave a defeated shrug. "Too bad it's going on the market. I'd buy it myself if I could afford it."

"It won't sell easily," Bridget said, and she should know. She'd been a real estate agent before she'd turned their family home into this inn. "Not many people can afford the upkeep on a place like that."

"Who owns it now that Martin Foster died?" Margo asked as she picked up a paper plate. There was a huge wooden tray of cheeses, green and red grapes, dried apricots, piles of nuts and sliced-up baguette, and crackers of all shapes and colors on the center of the table, nearly too pretty to pick at.

"A nephew apparently," Bridget said. She topped off her glass of white wine and passed the bottle to Abby.

Sarah chewed her lip. Chloe was staring intensely at the table. They were both thinking the same thing. There might be a way to please Hannah yet.

And there just might be a way to please Chloe, too, Sarah thought with a rush of hope. She set her glass of punch down on the table. Delicious as it was, she needed a clear head tonight. And tomorrow...Tomorrow would be a busy day. Tomorrow she would pay a visit to Crestview Manor and talk with this nephew. And by tomorrow night, everything might be right as rain...just not on a wedding day, of course.

Four

Sunday was Sarah's day off this week, but she may as well have been on the clock. She woke to her alarm, showered, dressed, and carefully did her hair and makeup, and then she drank a quick cup of coffee for liquid courage.

Crestview Manor was on the northern tip of town, a remote estate that was hidden behind a towering wrought-iron gate and a brick wall that seemed to be crumbling in places. The house itself was made of stone and covered in thick ivy. It was a heavy, solid house, not like the usual cedar-shingled capes and colonials that were widespread in these parts.

It was turning into a beautiful day, sunny, with just the right amount of ocean breeze to make her feel grateful that she lived in this small community, despite the lack of eligible bachelors, and Sarah rode her bike along the most scenic route, meandering up Shoreline Road, past the blooming blue and pink hydrangeas that spilled over white picket fences along the way. The shoreline was rockier up this way, and through a tall hedge of dense trees up ahead she finally spotted the property. Or estate. Or mansion. Whatever it was, from this viewpoint, it was breathtaking. It wasn't a beach house; there was nothing casual about it. The grounds were extensive and led to the sand. She couldn't imagine a better spot in Oyster Bay to get married. And, if it was up to her, Hannah would be doing just that.

She turned at the fork in the road and pedaled her way in the general direction of the house until the large gates appeared before her. She slowed, hopping off the seat and walking the bike the rest of the way, before propping it against the stone wall. She stared up at the gates, considering her options. She hadn't thought this far ahead, of course, and now she scanned the wall for some sort of intercom, but of course, there was none. The house was old, and it didn't appear to be updated with modern technology.

Finally, seeing no other option and unwilling to give up just yet, she gave a tentative push against the wrought iron, laughing at herself when it swung open without very much effort. Deciding to leave her bike in place for the time being, she straightened her shoulders and began the long walk on the gravel path toward the house. She had it all rehearsed. She would ring the bell, introduce herself, and pitch her services. That's right. Asking for a favor set the wrong tone. It would be much better if the current owner of the house interpreted her request as an honor. And really, what reason would he have to refuse?

It seemed to take minutes to finally reach the front

door. Or doors. They were of the double-set variety, wood and solid, but the doorjambs revealed paint that was flaking. There was at least a doorbell, and she pressed her finger to it, holding it there, hoping that it worked.

Evie was right. This house was old. Definitely in need of some sprucing up. But it was lovely. And the gardens... She smiled when she caught site of some bursting peonies that sprang from the grounds over to her left. A personal favorite. Once, she had been certain that peonies would make up her wedding bouquet.

Now she had accepted there would be no wedding bouquet at all. She was giving up.

She was just about to give up on waiting for someone to answer the door, too, and was considering walking around back to see if anyone was in the yard or on the beach, when there was a sound of a bolt turning and the door swung open.

A man not much older than herself with a thick head of brown hair and penetrating, deep-set brown eyes stared back at her. And he didn't look entirely happy to see her.

Sarah swallowed back her nerves. "Hello," she said, offering her best smile. She skirted her glance deeper into the house, waiting for a wife to appear in the distance. Perhaps she would be more receptive to the idea of a stunning wedding overlooking the expansive garden in less than three weeks?

But no wife appeared, and while normally this would have thrilled her to no end, today it troubled her. Almost as much as the frown that seemed etched on the man's face did.

"I'm Sarah Preston," she began. Damn. She'd forgotten her speech, and she'd worked so hard on it, perfecting it in her head into the late hours of the night and then again on the entire ride over here.

She waited to see if he would introduce himself, but he made no inclination. Perhaps he assumed she already knew him, or his name. She had come to his house, after all.

Now, perhaps sensing her hesitation, he arranged his features into something that bordered on polite interest, even if it was probably confusion. Even if it was noticeably of the impatient sort.

"I work for Bayside Brides, here in Oyster Bay," she went on. When he wasn't scowling he was actually quite good-looking, she decided. And younger than she'd first pegged him to be. She'd say he was thirty-two. Thirty-three tops. Her eyes betrayed her and dropped to his left hand, which gripped the brass doorknob as if he were ready to close the door on her at any moment.

No ring. Again something that would have once thrilled her. But not today. Nope. Today she was here on business matters. Nothing personal could interfere. Not again.

"I was hoping to speak to Marty Foster's nephew about renting out the garden for an upcoming wedding." Not exactly as poetic as she'd planned, but at least she got it out there in one breath.

"Did you know Marty?" he asked, catching her off

guard. It wasn't an inappropriate question, all things considered.

"No," she said, regrettably. "I'm still fairly new to this town." That was true, in a vague sense, and compared to all the townies who had lived here forever, a year and a half or so was relatively new. Still, she hoped he didn't ask for specifics. After all, it wasn't a good enough excuse for why she was at Marty Foster's home, asking to rent out the property, to save her hide.

Marty owed her no favors. This man blocking her path didn't either.

"The property isn't for rent," the man said gruffly. Then, after a hesitation, his mouth crooked into a strange sort of smile. "It is, however, for sale." His eyes seemed to hold hope in them as he looked at her.

She almost laughed. As if! Like anyone her age could afford such a property, and if they could, well, it was very obvious that it needed entirely far too much work. She could see the dust motes floating in the air behind him, and the tarps that were draping furniture in a room to his right. The overhead light fixture in the hallway (which could easily house her entire apartment) was covered in cobwebs.

"Are you the current owner?" she asked, hoping she wasn't being too forward. Still, she needed to know who she was dealing with here, and it was always better to go straight to the source. She'd learned that from Chloe, who never took no for an answer and who had made the impossible possible, because that was her job, she'd said. It was her job, she'd said, to make sure that every gown could be tailored to any bride. That the veils would be custom-ordered if need be. That the shoes would not give blisters. And, since she'd started planning weddings too, that every detail would be "personal, purposeful, and perfect." That was her motto.

Chloe had succeeded in all of this. But she hadn't succeeded in thwarting off a storm that had flooded Hannah's wedding venue. And Sarah knew that she had to succeed in securing Crestview Manor instead. She simply had to.

"I am Marty's nephew," he said. "Are you an interested buyer?"

She managed to cover her smile by glancing at the ground. "I'm afraid not," she said. "But I have a client who has always dreamed of getting married here, and she is happy to pay for the opportunity." She had a ballpark idea of what Hannah and Dan were refunded from the winery. She was ready to name the price if need be. First, though, she'd see what was offered.

"I'm sorry, but I'm only interested in selling the property at this time," the man said.

In other words, nothing was being offered.

"But we'll pay!" Sarah insisted, hating the twinge of desperation that sneaked into her tone. She hadn't rehearsed this far into things. The way she'd played it out in her mind, she'd make a reasonable argument and the person would be so flattered, that they would happily agree. After all, the house was just sitting here. It wouldn't sell anytime soon, and even then, closings would take a while. The wedding was only three weeks away. And they were willing to pay! "It's only for one night," she pleaded.

"The space is not available for rent," the man said, starting to close the door.

"Even for a wedding?" she asked, giving it one last try, but the look on the man's face told her she'd gone severely off-path.

His brow met in a stern gaze and his mouth set as he began to close the door. "*Especially* for a wedding," he said.

That evening, Sarah marched into Beads and Bobbles, Oyster Bay's beloved craft store, still cursing under her breath. She had a huge new speech she had prepared on the bike ride home—one she had started on the long walk back to the gates of the house—and one that she was now sure would have won over the grumpy new owner of Crestview.

She hadn't even caught his name.

"Hey there!" Kelly Myers grinned as Sarah approached the back table, where the knitting class she'd signed up for with Melanie was already underway. It was a coveted class, usually filled, and proof that Kelly had made the right choice in making Oyster Bay her new home.

Could Sarah say the same, she wondered, as she slid into the chair Melanie had saved for her, across from poor Ron, who was now such a masterful knitter, he could probably teach the class if Kelly ever got sick.

When Sarah had first moved from Bar Harbor, she'd sought out adventure and freedom. And she'd seen Oyster Bay as the perfect, pretty town to put down roots. Her parents had always been overprotective, an only child thing and all that, and they'd supported her decision to move away, mostly because her grandmother was close by, in Serenity Hills, the nursing home at the edge of town. It was a win-win, at least that's how it had felt originally. But now...

Nonsense, she told herself. She had a job she loved—at least for now. She had a wonderful group of friends, she had put down roots, and sure, it did stink to always be on the bridesmaid side of things, but would she rather have never met all these great women?

It was only that she'd hoped to meet a great man someday too.

"Sorry I'm late," she whispered to Melanie as she pulled her bamboo needles and yarn from her canvas tote. She'd spent the better part of the afternoon trying to think of a way to get the grumpy Foster heir to change his mind and lost track of time.

"It's open knitting today," Melanie reminded her, putting her anxiety at ease. She expertly added another row to the hat she was making.

Sarah stared down at her sad effort. She'd intended to make a winter set for her grandmother, but at the rate she was going, she'd be lucky to finish one mitten by Christmas, much less the hat or scarf.

She cast a glance at Ron's project. He was a fan of scarves when he was feeling low, what with his divorce now finalized and his ex-wife officially moving on with his coworker and all. But today he was whistling while he worked, and there was no scarf at all. Today he was making socks. Striped socks. With four different colored skeins of yarn.

With stern determination, she got to work. "I went over to Crestview Manor," she told Melanie.

"Crestview!" Melanie looked confused. "But why?"

Sarah pulled in a breath. She could tell Melanie anything, really, not that she had much to share right now. "I wanted to talk to the new owner. I was hoping he would let us rent out the place for Hannah's wedding."

"Oh, she would love that!" Kelly piped in, pulling up a stool beside them. "You know she was just so upset that the winery flooded. Of course, Chip offered up The Lantern, but it's not exactly what she had in mind for a wedding reception, and then Bridget offered up the inn, of course, but I still don't think Hannah's over the disappointment."

Despite all these setbacks, Kelly was beaming, and Sarah couldn't help it, she smiled too. Not long ago, Kelly had come to Oyster Bay to spend the holidays with her half-sister Hannah, and to meet her other half-sister, Evie, for the first time. She was tickled to be a bridesmaid. She managed to bring it up in every conversation.

"Did you know that the bridesmaids are carrying the mixed bouquets, too?" she told them, for at least the tenth time, but Melanie and Sarah just smiled politely.

"Oh, but of course you know! Chloe's planning the entire thing!"

"Hannah has excellent taste," Sarah said. She fumbled with the yarn, and without having to ask for help, Kelly took it from her hands, quickly fixed her error, and set the needles back on the table.

"There's nothing prettier than a summer bride," Melanie said.

Sarah gave her a funny look. "You say that about every bride, every season."

Melanie laughed. "True."

Kelly waggled her eyebrows. "Getting ideas for when you and Jason may tie the knot?"

"Please!" Melanie said, but her cheeks went all pink. "We're easing into things. We're not even talking about getting engaged."

Sarah added another row, trying to keep her concentration focused, and not just because she feared dropping another stitch. She had nothing to contribute to this conversation. Melanie and Kelly were both in love. They'd both found the one, whether they wanted to admit that or not, it was plain as day. They'd both be married within a year. Eighteen months for sure. Sarah would bet on that if she wasn't afraid that her next paycheck could be her last.

"So who is this new owner of Crestview?" Melanie finally said, changing the topic back to one that Sarah could relate to.

"Oh." She sighed with frustration as she set her

project down in her lap. "Just some guy with a chip on his shoulder."

Melanie's eyes flashed. "A guy? Like, how old?"

Sarah shrugged. "A little older than us."

She narrowed her eyes. Was that a knowing smile she saw pass between Melanie and Kelly?

"He's kind of a jerk," she clarified.

"Married?" Kelly asked. Her eyes seemed to gleam.

Sarah worked another row. It didn't look right. She was messing up because she didn't like where this conversation was going. Forcing a sigh, she shrugged. She didn't want to admit she had checked for a ring. "Didn't appear to be."

"So you'll give him a chance then!" Melanie was grinning as she knitted another row.

Sarah watched her fingers fly for a few moments. "He's not eligible. He's a jerk."

Melanie just waggled a finger at her. "You remember our deal..."

"What deal?" Kelly asked excitedly. Without asking, she reached out and took Sarah's project from her hands and began unraveling the last row. "You missed two stitches," she informed her.

Of course she had, because her mind was on anything but Grandma Esther's Christmas gift. Her mind was on the mystery man at Crestview Manor. The heir, she supposed.

He *was* handsome. But unpleasant. Yes, quite unpleasant! And she was finished falling for men based solely on their good looks.

"Sarah says that she has given up on love," Melanie informed Kelly, who looked at Sarah as if she had lost her mind. "And so I challenged her to stop seeking out the same kinds of guys she always falls for—you know, the noncommittal types. To force herself to give the very next guy she met a chance, even if she didn't feel sparks right away."

"I didn't feel sparks," Sarah was sure to say, but Melanie didn't meet her eye.

"Sounds like fair advice," Kelly said, handing Sarah back the mitten and knitting needles.

"It does," Sarah admitted. "In theory." And the truth was that he was single, of the right age, and not hard on the eye. And he was the gatekeeper to the flower garden and terrace with the sweeping view of the sea, large enough to hold a large tent, should the weather decide to not cooperate.

"So you'll give him another chance?" Melanie asked hopefully.

Sarah went back to her project. She'd give him another chance, all right, but not in the way that Melanie intended. She'd win him over, ensure that he let them rent out the space for Hannah's wedding.

After all, her love life may have no future, but her career sure as heck had to have one.

Five

Room service at the Oyster Bay Hotel was one of the only perks that Chris saw to staying in this town another week. This morning he'd gone for the Belgian waffle with a side of eggs, bacon, and hash browns, something that Jenna would have frowned over, something that still made him feel guilty as he scraped the plate, taking in one last bite. But then, a decadent breakfast wasn't the only thing to feel bad about when it came to Jenna.

He stepped away from the table near the window, where the sunlight filtered through the drapes, eager to get a start on his day nearly as much as he dreaded the thought of returning to that old house. He'd made some progress over the weekend, but not enough, and the truth was that he wasn't so sure he'd be able to get it all done in time for an estate sale this weekend. By five o'clock yesterday, when the dust in the air was so thick that his eyes were burning and he saw little, if any, actual change to the naked eye, he considered calling on Janice to help him out. But that wouldn't be fair. After all, Janice had been getting on in years the last time he'd visited. He couldn't in good conscience put her to work now, not when she was probably enjoying a much-earned retirement.

No, Crestview Manor was his problem, and his alone. But it had been a burden long before now.

He checked his watch, cursing that he'd wasted time over something as leisurely as breakfast when he'd hoped to get an early start. But the food would help him to power through, and the delay, well, he didn't need a shrink to tell him that he was procrastinating, putting off another day in that house, alone with nothing but the memories.

With his laptop in hand, he opened the door to the hall and made his way to the elevator bank. The hotel seemed quiet; most people had probably cleared out last night, after a relaxing weekend getaway. Oyster Bay wasn't exactly a destination for businessmen throughout the week. Hoping that this was the case, he made his way to the business center in the lobby of the hotel, happy to see that the computer docking stations were empty. In no time, he was able to print a few dozen copies of the flyers he'd created to advertise this weekend's estate sale. Jeff had left a message yesterday when Chris was knee-deep in cobwebs, saying that he'd already listed the house on the MLS and would send a photographer over early this week to take some shots of the house for the listing.

It was a warm morning, the kind of morning that made Chris want to play hooky, from work, from the tasks at hand, and escape for a bit. But relaxation had never quite been his thing, and besides, he couldn't afford to waste another week tending to this old house when he had a real job to get back to. A real life to get back to—sort of, he thought, forcing himself down the street.

Technically, he was allowed a vacation. Technically, he could afford a vacation. He worked for himself. He set his own schedule. His clients would understand one week off, surely.

But he didn't like to relax. Didn't like to slow down. It was better to keep busy. Keep moving. One foot in front of the other.

His first stop was a café named Angie's that he hoped had a bulletin board he could use. Sure enough, he had barely crossed the threshold into the vestibule when he was greeted with a crowded board advertising everything from knitting classes to babysitters. He found a spare tack and placed his sign front and center.

"You know, you're covering that volunteer sign-up sheet for the summer festival," a voice behind him said.

He turned, prepared to stake his claim, after all, his sheet was barely covering one inch of the corner of any other poster, and he was hardly the first offender, but his defenses came down when he caught the eye of the woman who had shown up at his door yesterday morning. She was holding a paper cup of coffee, and she was smiling at him.

"Oh. Well." He flicked his eyes back to the board and then returned them to her. She was pretty. Prettier than he'd remembered, with blonde hair and a perky smile, and it had been one of his first impressions of her yesterday, along with complete irritation at being interrupted. "Just the corner. I mean, I could move it."

She grinned wider. Her blue eyes seemed to gleam. It was then that he realized she was having fun with him. "It's fine. Besides, that sign-up sheet is at least a month old. Someone just forgot to take it down. Angie gets busy, and Leah is always at the counter, and neither of them wants to upset anyone by taking down their postings, so unless the people who tack up these items come along and remove them, well, they tend to remain."

Geez, she was chatty. He cleared his throat. "Good to know."

Her coffee smelled good, and he hoped to push past her into the café and grab one of his own before he moved on to the next spot on Main Street. But the woman moved forward, peering at the sign, her shoulder brushing his as she got a better look at the fine print.

He froze, wondering if she would move away, or if he should, but he found himself easing into the sensation, standing there, so close he could feel the rise and fall of her breath and smell her perfume. Something sweet. Inviting.

Or maybe it was just something being baked in the café's kitchen.

Right. He did back away this time. Just an inch.

Her gaze was sharp on his. "An estate sale, huh?" She sipped her coffee, waiting for him to respond. "Clearing out some of the items in the house?"

"I have no need for any of that stuff," he said a little gruffly. Most of the items in the house were old, antiques, dating back to when his grandparents had lived there, and his grandfather's parents before that. Marty loved the old stuff. He appreciated it. He liked to hold onto the past.

Chris felt his jaw pulse.

"There's an antique shop down the street," the woman offered. She took another sip of her coffee, eyeing him over the rim of her paper cup. "I bet they could give you a quote. There's probably a lot of value in some of those old pieces."

She raised a good point, but top dollar wasn't what he was after. Still, he'd be sure to stop into the shop she had mentioned, to let them know about the sale. They might be a good customer next weekend, or tell a few collectors about it, too. He'd love nothing more than to clear the place out before he left town and never have to think about it again.

"Thanks, I'll stop in, but I'm more interested in clearing everything out quickly."

The woman nodded but didn't seem to take the hint. "So you're putting the house up for sale then?"

He shrugged. He wasn't sure what Marty intended him to do with the property, and that unsettled him. He told himself that Marty had no one else to leave it to. But when he thought of it like that, he felt the weight of pressure on his shoulders that he had to do right by it. Marty knew that if he left it to Chris's father, he would just turn around and sell it. Did he expect something different from Chris? Or did he just assume that Chris should have some say, after all the time he'd spent there?

"It's a little big for just one person," he said finally, which was true, very true, or so he liked to tell himself. After all, Marty had lived there alone for years.

"Well." She cleared her throat. Her cheeks seemed to have gone a little pink. "You know, if you walk a few blocks down Main to the offices of the Oyster Bay Gazette, you may be able to take out an ad in the paper." Perhaps sensing his hesitation, she added, "They have an online version that gets a lot of traffic from neighboring communities."

He had to admit that this was yet another good idea on her part. "Thanks," he said, genuinely appreciating it. "I think I'll do that."

"Tell them I sent you," she said. Then, because his expression must have revealed his confusion, she added, "Sarah Preston. I used to work there."

Sarah. Now he remembered. Remembered something else too.

"You used to work there before becoming a wedding planner?" He arched a brow. If she was hoping to change his mind about the wedding she wanted to host on the property, she was wasting her time.

"Technically I work for Bayside Brides," she said. "We're a bridal salon but we're branching into event planning, too."

Hence the reason she was looking for a venue for an upcoming wedding. He saw this as his cue to exit.

Sarah, it seemed, had other ideas.

"I'm actually headed your way," she informed him. "Bayside Brides is across the street and down a ways. I can walk with you."

He couldn't mask his discomfort with this, even though he knew he was overreacting. He'd grown too used to being alone in recent years, slowly drifting away from friends, finding excuses to avoid social interactions. Heck, he didn't even have to go into an office. He worked from his home, and the fact that his clients were located all across the country meant that he could technically work from anywhere. But he had a routine that worked. He woke at six, went for a five-mile run, came home, showered, dressed, and brought his one and only mug of coffee into the room he'd set up with a large desk and two oversized computer screens. He emerged for lunch, and then again for dinner. Lunch was usually something microwaveable. Dinner was take-out or delivery. He didn't have any pets. He only knew the names of a few of the neighbors in his building, and even then, he'd wished he didn't. Stan, the sweet, older man who lived across the hall, was forever trying to set Chris up with his grand-daughter. Poor Stan didn't know the half of it, and Chris certainly didn't feel like sharing.

He was thirty-three years old. People saw him as a bachelor, someone who might be shy about committing, or even reluctant. They had no idea that he was a widower. That he had committed. Been there, done that.

No looking back. Just forward.

"Lead the way," he said, forcing a grin that he didn't feel. His expression felt tight, unnatural, but if Sarah noticed, she didn't let on. She was just being friendly, welcoming, even, and really, what was so wrong with that?

This was a small town. This was probably normal around here. Talking to people. Interacting with people.

No wonder Marty had been a recluse. It was probably the only way to ensure any privacy in this town.

Sarah didn't realize she was smiling until Melanie pointed it out. The bells were still clanging, the door to the shop had barely closed behind her, and Melanie was standing behind the counter, looking at her with keen interest that told Sarah that she must have been watching more than Sarah just walking through the door. No doubt she had also caught her walking up to the door with a man. A good-looking man. Of the right age.

He did have a nice smile, she thought. There was a slight dimple on his left cheek. It was endearing, and it made him seem almost approachable. But not quite. He was guarded, and his defenses were up. They wouldn't easily come down, she feared, but she'd still try. In the professional sense.

"Don't you look happy!" Melanie remarked.

Sarah could only shake her head. "Don't go reading into things." After all, right up until she had run into the Foster heir at Angie's, she had all but lost her breakfast, so great were her nerves at the thought of today's looming Monday meeting, and the ominous suggestion that Chloe had made over the weekend that they would be discussing her professional indiscretion today.

Was it too much to hope that Chloe may have forgotten?

"So was that him?" Melanie waggled her eyebrows as she closed the jewelry display case.

"The nephew of Marty Foster? Yes." Chris Foster. He'd finally revealed his name on their brief walk, and only because she'd asked. He wasn't exactly the warm and fuzzy type. Not exactly sending out vibes of any sort of interest, in any shape or form.

"Seemed like you two were getting along just fine today," Melanie said airily.

Sarah set her hands on her hips and gave her friend a long look. "Why are you so determined to see me give this guy a chance?" Really! Of all people! Melanie shouldn't be too encouraged by his outward appearance. Sarah wasn't. Not entirely, at least.

She shook her head as she made her way to the storage room to hang up her bag, but Melanie stopped her before she could push through the door. "Chloe is in there," she warned. "With Hannah."

Sarah frowned. Chloe never let clients into the storage room! Sure, it was bright, with crisp white shelving and a long table in the center that doubled as a workspace. The walls were two shades lighter than the blue in the storefront. But there was a kitchenette. There was a bulletin board with memos tacked to it in a less-than-organized fashion. There was a houseplant that had seen better days.

"You didn't tell her about me trying to convince the Foster nephew to let us use Crestview for the wedding, did you?" She chewed her thumb worriedly. The last thing she needed was to be giving false hope on top of everything else, or have Chloe thinking that she was over-stepping.

But to her relief, Melanie shook her head. "No. I didn't think it was my place."

"Good." Sarah nodded, breathing only a little easier. "If you talk to Kelly today, can you ask her not to say anything either? I don't think that he's going to come around, and I'd hate to lift Hannah's spirits just to have them come crashing down again." After all, she knew that feeling all too well.

"Certainly." Melanie gave a perfunctory nod of agreement. "I'm sure Kelly will agree."

That was one potential problem solved, at least. "So we aren't having our Monday meeting then?" They used to be later, over lunch, but with how busy they were lately, Chloe had pushed them up into the morning. Now, she wondered if Chloe might find they were too busy to have a weekly meeting at all. She noted the hope in her voice, which was quickly shot down again when Melanie shook her head.

"Hannah came in early, before work. It makes sense for us to use the time that the retail shop isn't open for our other services. I think Chloe will touch on that more in the meeting."

The meeting. Why did one word make her stomach heave?

"Chloe wants to start using the storage room space for meetings," Melanie said. "She said it was easier than going over things here on the sofa and chairs. She stayed late last night sprucing things up."

Sarah had to agree that this was probably a better use for the space. It was a large room, and there was a table where they could spread out their ideas.

Happy for the delay, Sarah waited until Melanie walked over to the dressing rooms before she settled into the seat at the counter and checked on the status of all their outstanding orders, so she would have something useful to report when the meeting started.

When that was finished, she went through the inventory, making notes for anything that needed to be reordered. They kept a few things in stock at all times, available for immediate purchase, while other items in the shop were samples. She started with the shoes. Even though most of these had to be ordered in specific sizes, they also liked to keep at least four sizes of each style on hand. She checked on the strappy kitten heels, available in pearl, white, champagne, and gold. She jotted a note to herself on her clipboard that they were low on size seven.

The door to the back room opened as Sarah moved toward the veils, trying not to think about Jane Merrik and how badly she had messed up on Friday.

"The Harper House Inn is a beautiful location," Chloe was saying, even though her tone seemed strained. "That view!"

Hannah pulled a face. She sighed, clearly disappointed. "I know. It's just that both Bridget and Margo were married there. And it's their home more than mine. And it's just not what I wanted. I know it will be lovely, but I'd wanted something more of my own."

Sarah fluffed a few of the veils. They had plenty in stock, and those orders were usually custom anymore. Lots of brides wanted a specific clip or length or trim. There was no way they could keep enough options on hand to please everyone.

"It will be your own," Chloe said, tapping her clipboard. "I promise."

Hannah gave a resigned wave to Sarah and said goodbye to Melanie as she left the shop. Chloe's shoulders seemed to visibly sag as she stared out the window onto Main Street.

"Should we start our meeting now?" Melanie came out from the dressing rooms, where she'd set out a few dresses for the afternoon clients on the schedule, and glanced over at Sarah, who now felt positively sick with nerves. Chloe was already in a bad mood. This certainly didn't bode well for the meeting.

"I see no reason to delay it," Chloe said, leading them back through the open door to the room which had indeed been spruced up overnight. In the center of the table was a row of three small flower arrangements in varying shades of pink, a larger one had been set up on the long shelf against the wall, which used to house overstuffed folders of purchase orders and invoices and which now held lovely baskets and a row of wedding books with candy-colored spines.

The kitchenette had been cleaned up. There was now

water and coffee at the ready, for clients, Sarah gathered.
And the bulletin board was now covered with inspira-
tional seasonal photos of centerpieces, wedding invitations, and cake displays.

"This is gorgeous!" Sarah marveled. She couldn't
help it; she felt excited. When she had come on board at
Bayside Brides, this was exactly the type of opportunity
she had been seeking. The chance to put her creative
visions to work, to see them come to life.

Chloe said nothing as she slid into her usual chair.
Melanie and Sarah followed suit.

"We had a call from Jane Merrik this morning,"
Chloe said, looking at Sarah across the table.

Sarah felt the air leave her lungs, and Melanie had
gone so still beside her that she was relatively certain that
her friend had stopped breathing as well at this news.

"She's decided not to move forward with us."

"What?" Sarah couldn't disguise her shock. "But
that's ridiculous. I made a flippant comment—"

"A comment that made her want to take her business
elsewhere," Chloe said, raising an eyebrow. "The planning of the wedding is just as special to some brides as the
wedding itself. It's a once-in-a-lifetime opportunity.
Something that they've waited for all their lives."

And Sarah had cast a dark cloud over it. She understood. "I'm sorry. I never would have said anything if I
knew a client was present. You know how much I love
working here."

"Do I?" Chloe surprised her by saying. She shook her
head, causing her low, blonde ponytail to swish over her

shoulders. "I need to know that you believe in the product you're selling. We can't sell someone a wedding dress that we don't believe will make them feel absolutely beautiful."

"But, of course I believe that! You know I've been subscribing to wedding magazines since I was a kid! I know all the designers. I follow the trends. I want to be a part of this business, Chloe."

Sarah glanced over at Melanie, who looked pained. Chloe said nothing for what felt like several excruciating minutes, even though it was probably only seconds. Long ones.

"Why don't you take a few days off? Gather yourself. Tend to whatever personal issues you have. Then we can decide if Bayside Brides is the right fit for you."

Sarah felt the blood drain from her face. Her mouth felt dry, and she chose her next words very carefully. "But it is the right fit for me. I'm sure of it. I messed up. It won't happen again."

"You're right. It won't. Mistakes are one thing. Attitude is another. We'll regroup next week."

Next week. Did Chloe mean it? She wanted Sarah to leave? What about the storefront? Who would cover the walk-ins when Melanie was meeting with a bride for a custom gown and Chloe was meeting with Jessie for the invitations or Posy for the flowers?

But from the patient way that Chloe was watching her, waiting for her, she knew that Chloe was dead serious. Without looking at either of her bosses, Sarah stood, and walked out of the back room and into the storefront, barely remembering to grab her handbag from under the counter as she moved to the door, as calmly yet quickly as she could on shaking legs.

Her eyes blurred from tears, but she didn't let them spill. Couldn't let them spill.

She pushed out of the shop and into the sunshine, feeling the warmth on her face. In the short time she'd been inside, the street had come to life. It was summer. Kids were out, getting ready for a long day at the beach.

Melanie called out to her before she could reach the corner. Reluctantly, Sarah turned, even though she knew it wasn't Melanie's fault at all.

"She just needs to cool off. Losing the Merrik wedding was a big blow, and she's already losing sleep over letting Hannah down."

"And I feel terrible!" Sarah cried. "It was never my intention."

"I know that, and so does she, deep down." Melanie squeezed her arm. "Show her that you believe in love again. That you are still that hopeless romantic we first brought into the shop."

Sarah understood what Melanie was saying, but how was she supposed to convince her when the truth was that she wasn't that same girl anymore. The old Sarah did believe that there was a perfect match out there for everyone, that if two people were meant to be, they would find a way. The old Sarah cried over television movies. She was a sap. Somehow she had to find her way back to that.

"I believe in giving the brides the best day they can

have," she said. "I believe that every wedding should be beautiful, and I can help make it that way."

"I think you believe in more than that," Melanie said. "It was what made Chloe so eager to hire you." She reached down and squeezed Sarah's hand. "Take some time. Get over this disappointment with online dating. And remember our deal. Give the next guy you meet a fair chance. Opening your heart to the idea of love and happy endings will go a long way in winning back Chloe's support."

Sarah nodded along, even though her heart wasn't in it.

The Foster nephew had potential, all right. But her mission was purely professional.

Six

The next morning Sarah woke to the sound of birds chirping outside her window instead of the ringing of her alarm. She was out of coffee, because she usually grabbed one on the way to work, and because Monday afternoons were typically when she went grocery shopping too, and yesterday, the last thing she wanted to do was linger in public any longer than necessary.

What if she ran into a client? How would she explain her sudden absence from the shop? What if she ran into that busybody Dottie Joyce, who would question why she was grocery shopping in the middle of the day instead of fluffing tulle at Bayside Brides, or ask why she was wearing her sunglasses indoors?

No one could see the tears. It was too small of a town. No one could know about her indiscretion if she wanted to ever keep her credibility.

She still had a job, she told herself, over and over, even though it was not exactly comforting. It technically could be worse, she knew. And Melanie would fight for her. But she had to hold up her end of the bargain, too. She had to find a way to believe in love again.

She just didn't know how when it seemed that the only emotion she ever had to associate with romance anymore was complete and utter disappointment.

Because she saw no reason to sit around her apartment feeling sorry for herself, she dressed and went into town, deciding if anyone asked, she would claim she was taking the day off to visit her grandmother, which she just might, and probably should do. She bypassed Angie's in case Chloe popped in for a latte and headed to Books by the Bay instead, where the owner, Trish McDowell, sold coffee, tea, and scones in addition to the latest juicy paperbacks.

Maybe she'd pick up a romance novel to get her back into the spirit of things. Trish kept a bunch of them on hand at the front table, especially anything by JR Anderson, now an Oyster Bay resident and husband to Bridget Harper, who happened to be one of Trish's best friends since childhood.

Trish was also married to Jeff, who, according to Bridget, was representing the sale of Crestview Manor. Sarah decided to feel out the situation. See if something useful could be gleaned that might help her change Chris Foster's mind about letting them rent out the space for a night. A single night. Really, what was the problem?

"Hi, Trish," she said, smiling as she wandered to the back of the room.

Trish blew a wisp of hair from her forehead and set a

stack of books on the counter. "How are you, Sarah? How's your grandmother?"

It was no secret that Sarah's grandmother had been recently diagnosed with Alzheimer's, and while she didn't like to think about her grandmother growing older, or what her future held, she appreciated Trish's concern.

"I think she's finally stopped asking Dr. Sawyer to marry her," Sarah said brightly, and Trish laughed. When Jason Sawyer had moved back to town and taken over his father's clinic, he had made quite an impression on Esther Preston, and Sarah knew that her grandmother looked nearly as forward to his weekly visits to her at Serenity Hills as she did Sarah's visits.

"I'm so happy that Jason and Melanie are together," Trish said as she sorted the books into two piles. "Do you think there's any chance of them getting married?"

"Oh, no doubt. They were made for each other." After all, it had been plain as day when Sarah met Jason that he only had eyes for Melanie, even though Melanie had been completely oblivious. It had taken everything in Sarah not to take her friend by the shoulders and give her a good, hard shake. What was Melanie doing pining around about that jerk Doug McKinney, who had broken up with her on Valentine's Day of all days, when the perfect man was right in front of her?

Sarah smiled to herself. Maybe Melanie was right. Maybe it would be a good idea to look past the obvious and open her mind. After all, she was just as much prey to the smooth talkers as Melanie had once been.

Still, Chris Foster was not the man. He was too... grumpy, too guarded. Too...something.

Trish gave a small smile as she sorted through the titles in her stack. "Every pot has its lid, as the saying goes!"

Yes. Well. Sarah used to believe in phrases like this too until recently. But what if her lid was traveling around China, living in Florida, or dating someone else? All she knew was that her lid was not in Oyster Bay, and that she wasn't going to keep trying on different lids until she found one that fit. She could search forever. She already felt like she'd searched forever. She was tired. She was, admittedly, jaded.

"I suppose," she sighed. She was an ambassador for Bayside Brides, after all. Even though she may not be in the shop today, buttoning up the backs of dresses, or adjusting hem lengths with pins, she wasn't taking any more chances when it came to diplomacy. She had to believe in the dream she was selling—that's what Chloe had said... She had to believe in happy endings. That meant she had to believe that Hannah Donovan had a chance at getting the wedding of her dreams.

She decided to cut to the point of coming in here today, other than for the coffee, which she had almost forgotten about.

"Bridget told us that the Crestview Manor estate has gone on the market."

Trish raised her eyebrows. "So Jeff told me. Between you and me, I don't know if that will sell anytime soon."

Sarah gave her a knowing look. "It needs a lot of work. Maybe it's a teardown?"

"It can't be," Trish surprised her by saying. "It's a registered historical landmark. No major changes without approval. And it most certainly cannot be demolished."

Sarah considered this information. It wasn't surprising, not given the age and size of the place. It had once been beautiful, and it still was, in its own charming way. She thought of Hannah, who saw something in it that other people might, too.

"Surely a buyer might love the property, though. It's not easy to come by oceanfront land like that."

"We'll see," Trish sighed, but she didn't look very convinced. She picked up the shorter pile of books and pressed them against her chest. "The seller is quite motivated, so I imagine whoever is lucky enough to buy it can get it for a steal." Trish wandered into the children's section and pushed a book between two others on an already crammed shelf.

Sarah followed her, not quite ready to drop this topic just yet.

"I'm surprised that the owner would be willing to part with the house," she commented as she trailed Trish deeper into the pastel-colored extension off the back of the shop. It was decorated with a summer theme, and large construction paper cutouts of beach balls and umbrellas dotted the space above the shelves.

"It was his uncle's house," Trish remarked. "Jeff said that he spent every summer here in Oyster Bay. Jeff remembers him vaguely."Trish skirted her eyes to Sarah, narrowing them slightly. "Have you met this Chris Foster?"

"I did meet him. He was hanging up signs for an estate sale this weekend." Not exactly the full truth, but no need to elaborate on her little appearance at his door on Sunday.

"Oh, yes. The estate sale. It should help clear things out, at least. Marty never could part with anything, and antiques don't usually appeal to new buyers." Trish tucked the last of the books into its place on the shelf and then turned to face Sarah. "But if you ask me, that's too big of a project for one person. And if he wants to sell that place anytime soon, he'll need all the help he can get."

Sarah felt her lips curl into a smile as the first swell of real hope she'd had in a while filled her. So Chris needed a bit of help, did he?

Lucky for her, she had all the time in the world this week.

The doorbell rang just as Chris was pulling the tarp off a Chesterfield leather sofa. He coughed as the dust swirled up in the air and set the tarp in the pile with the others.

"Just a minute!" he called as he moved out into the hallway, even though he doubted very much that anyone could hear him through the door. It was solid, just like the rest of this house. But still, judging from the paint peeling from its frame, it had seen better days.

He wiped the sweat from his brow with the back of his hand and opened the door, expecting to see the gardener, whom he'd called that morning, after rifling through Marty's desk for the number. Instead, he saw that pesky wedding planner. A nice enough woman, but still. Pesky.

"Sarah, right?" He kept his expression pleasant but specifically uninterested. He didn't have time for chitchat right now. He had tarps to remove, dusting to do, a vacuum to locate, and windows to wash. And that leaky faucet to fix, and he wasn't much of a handyman.

"I hope I'm not interrupting you." She smiled up at him, and he fought back a wave of impatience. She most certainly was interrupting him—again—but he was far too polite to say so directly.

He shifted the weight on his feet. "Just tackling the old place. There's a lot to do if I'm going to get out of here by the end of the weekend." In other words, *hint, hint*. In other words, please go and leave him to it.

"That's why I'm here," she said, surprising him. "I can help."

He didn't manage to repress his sigh this time. Holding up a hand, he said, "You've helped enough. The newspaper...the antiques shop. All great ideas. Thank you." He set his jaw. *Now please leave*, he willed her.

"No, I mean, with the house. I'm sure there's a lot to do to get it ready for this weekend's estate sale. I have some time on my hands this week."

He frowned at her. "Are you serious?"

"Completely serious," she said brightly. She roved her eye up and down him and then grinned. "Looks like the place is dusty."

It was dusty, and he did need help, badly. But something didn't ring true here. His eyes narrowed. "Why would you help me? You don't even know me."

She shrugged, her smile not even slipping. "We like to help people out in Oyster Bay. It's a tight community like that."

True, all true, but a random act of kindness like this didn't come along without some strings. He was a shrewd businessman, not a dummy.

"I've got it covered, but thanks," he said, reaching for the doorknob.

She held out her hand, stopping him. He would have been amused if he wasn't so annoyed. The woman drove a hard bargain, and something told him that she wasn't finished with her pitch just yet.

"I hear it will be a tough sale," she commented. When he frowned in response to that, she added, "It's a small town. People talk."

"You heard right," he said. He could just imagine what the upkeep of this place would be, year after year, if it sat vacant. He felt a headache coming on. And this time, it wasn't from the dust.

"And I imagine that the estate sale this weekend might be the best surge of traffic to come through this place for a while."

Again, she had him there. His patience was thinning,

and time was getting away from him. Time she was reminding him that he didn't have.

He managed a thin smile. "What is it that you want, Ms. ..." He'd forgotten again, or maybe he hadn't been paying close enough attention. Didn't want to pay attention. But it was being forced on him. Over and over again. She wasn't going to give up, he realized.

"Preston," she finished. "Am I really that forgettable?" She grinned, rather cheekily, and despite his reservations, he found himself warming up to her.

"What is it that you're asking for in exchange for helping me to fix up this house for the estate sale?" He folded his arms across his chest, waiting for it.

She licked her lower lip, and, without being invited, stepped inside the foyer, forcing him to take a step back. "Now, just hear me out, for two minutes, and if we don't reach an agreement, I'll go, and I'll leave you to all... this..." She motioned to the peeling paint on the doorframes, the fading wallpaper, and the cobwebs on the sconces that flanked a dingy mirror. "I'll leave you to handle *all* of this *all* on your own."

Was that a glimmer of amusement he saw pass through her eyes? He managed to firm his mouth before his smile gave him away. She was savvy. Feisty. But damn, she was pesky.

"Two minutes," he said, and that was being generous. Still, he was growing curious, and he had to admit that listening to her spiel was better than scrubbing tile grout —at least for a few minutes.

Her eyes flashed in surprise, giving her away for one

telling second. She hadn't expected that any more than he'd expected an offer of help to appear at his doorway. An offer he very much needed, especially considering the cleaning crew he'd called said they were booked up two weeks out. "Tourist season," they'd said. He'd offered them double. They'd only laughed.

"Okay. So." She held up her hands like she was framing a picture and moved to the back of the hall, all the way through to the back of the house where the large, glass-enclosed conservatory opened up, giving a panoramic view of the terrace and flowering garden. It was probably one of the nicest rooms in the house, with the paned windows and doors and the lush greenery shadowing it just enough to keep the temperature cooler than one might expect in a house without air-conditioning.

"Picture it," she said, splaying her hands in the air. "Chairs set up here, forming an aisle. A trellis set up there, between the rose bushes. A bride, her eyes shining with tears of joy, gracefully walking through the crowd of guests to unite with her one true love."

Her eyes cut to him. He kept his expression purposefully blank.

She pinched her lips. Went back to business. "A string quartet will be sitting there, off to the corner near the carriage house. A salty breeze blows in off the ocean, rustling the bride's veil. Everyone watches on bated breath as they take their vows, right here, on this special property that the bride and groom have chosen as the place where the most sacred of—"

He couldn't take another minute of this. "Okay, I get it," he said, holding up a hand.

"It would be a beautiful wedding," she urged him. "And the bride has dreamed of getting married here since she was a little girl."

He pulled in a breath. Guilt wouldn't work with him. He had enough of it weighing on him already.

"And I'd oversee everything," she said quickly. "Well, along with the other women I work with. You wouldn't have to do anything. No work. No cleaning. You wouldn't even know we were here."

He shifted the weight on his feet. She was never going to sell him on this wedding. But he could be bought on her other suggestion. "The help you offered. How much of it are you offering?"

Her eyes sprung open. "Through the week! And the weekend! I can help with the estate sale, too. From now through Sunday, you can consider me *completely* at your service."

"Fine," he said, knowing that he would live to regret this but not seeing much choice. After all, it wasn't like he would be here when the wedding took place. He'd be back in Boston. Back in his life. Away from this house and all the memories it stirred up.

"If you'll just hear me out—Wait. Did you say *yes*? Did you say we could have the wedding here?"

He was going to regret this, he feared, but what choice did he have? He needed help, and she was offering it.

"You can have the wedding here. One wedding. But

be prepared to pay for it," he chuckled. "You won't want to be getting that dress all dusty," he said, pointing to the blue sundress she wore that hugged her curves and skimmed just above her knees, revealing long, smooth legs. He looked away, swallowing hard.

"You said yes! You said yes!" She whooped with delight, and, before he knew what was happening, flung her arms around his neck. He closed his eyes, for one brief moment, smelling honey and vanilla and feeling the silky whoosh of hair against his cheek.

Just as quickly, it was over. She pulled back. Her cheeks were on fire. She was so close he could see the blueness of her eyes, the dusting of freckles on her nose.

"Sorry. I got carried away for a minute there."

And so had he. He righted himself. Cleared his throat. Pushed back the swell in his chest that was a strange mix of longing and regret. "So I take it you agree to the arrangement then?"

She blinked several times. "Absolutely. I'll help you fix this place up and we can use the space two weeks from Saturday for a wedding."

"Deal." He held out his hand, and she slipped hers into it. She had a good grip, but there was still something soft and smooth and a reminder that it had been a long time since he'd touched another woman, and never on this terrace.

He stiffened. "I'll see you tomorrow morning then."

She nodded. "Tomorrow morning."

He should say this afternoon, seeing as the day was young and she could go home and change, but he needed to clear his head. Needed to get back to work. Tomorrow he'd be ready for her.

"Well, then." He backed up, toward the house, wondering why he was suddenly looking so forward to tomorrow when he'd been dreading the thought of coming to this house every day this week. "Tomorrow."

"You won't regret this," she said as she walked away, toward the side of the house. "I'm a hard worker."

"I gathered that," he said, laughing softly.

He was still smiling when he went back into the house, and before he could close the glass French doors of the conservatory, he heard a noise that made him jump so hard that he nearly took the handle off.

It wasn't until he saw Sarah toss herself into a cartwheel that made her dress fly up just enough to reveal a peek of her thighs that he realized that the squeal had come from here, and not from that mouse that he was near certain he had heard scampering around in the attic.

Seven

The next morning Sarah woke to her alarm, grateful for the purpose to her day. It was taking everything in her not to pick up the phone and call Chloe and blurt the good news, but she didn't want to jinx herself—or get ahead of herself, which she had been known to do. What if she showed up today and Chris decided he had changed his mind? It wouldn't be the first time a man had done that to her.

No cynical talk, she told herself. After all, that was exactly what had landed her in this mess in the first place.

She put on jeans and a tank top and pulled her hair into a ponytail. She would have loved to slide into her cute pink suede flip-flops with the bow near the toe, but they weren't very practical for deep cleaning, so she put on her gym shoes instead, reminding herself that it wasn't like she needed to impress the guy or anything—it wasn't a *date*. She was ready to roll up her sleeves, if she had any. So she was wearing a smidgen of lipstick. She deserved to look her best at all times, didn't she?

Still, she fought back the excitement that filled her as she rode her bike to Crestview. It was just the excitement of scoring a win for Chloe and Hannah, she told herself. The relief of finding a reason to keep her job. The simple joy of seeing her friend have the wedding of her dreams.

It had absolutely nothing to do with the promise of a day spent in the company of a single, attractive man of the right age bracket. He was grumpy and stiff and so not her type.

And she was not even going to think about what Melanie would have to say about that.

"Hey." Chris greeted her with a smile and held the door open for her to pass.

My, what a difference from the last time, she thought as she crossed the threshold into the incredibly dusty house. She sneezed. And then she sneezed again. Four times in a row.

Make that five.

Her eyes were watering. No doubt her mascara was starting to run. She knew she shouldn't have worn any, but... But nothing. She was here to work. Physical labor! She was not here to flirt or even to hope to flirt.

Chris winced by way of apology. "I'm afraid the house has been abandoned for some time. I haven't visited in a while, and my uncle was in Serenity Hills the last few years of his life."

"My grandmother lives there." Sarah subtly wiped the mascara from under her eyes. She sensed something ease in him, the tension release from his face. Something in common then. "I'm surprised she never hit on him."

He laughed in surprise. "What?"

Sarah shrugged, but she was smiling too. "My grandmother got a little man crazy for a while there. Last I checked, she's still at it. She's not very particular about age, so if you ever run into her, don't be shocked if she asks you to marry her."

His eyes gleamed with amusement but he just shook his head. "You don't need to worry about that. I have no intention of ever marrying."

And there it was. She didn't know why she should feel the weight of disappointment settle in her chest, but it did, like the final nail, the harsh reminder of why she was in this predicament in the first place. She didn't believe that she would find the one, and Melanie's silly challenge wouldn't change her mind. She didn't meet any men who were looking for the same things that she was. And Chris was just one of the same. If she'd let herself, she could have fallen for him too, dared to hope and wish for things that weren't on the table and would never materialize.

Really, how could Chloe blame her for bursting into work and saying that she'd given up?

"So, where should we start?" she asked. She'd left her handbag at home and she was happy that she had. There was nowhere to set anything. The floors were covered in a layer of dust nearly as thick as the light fixtures. From the rooms that she could see off the hall, most furniture was still covered in tarps. Paint seemed to be chipping from doorframes, and wallpaper was peeling in the corners. It was almost impossible to take in the beauty and scale of the place when the condition was so overwhelming.

"I've been going room by room," Chris said. He ran a hand through his hair as he led her through the first floor. Sarah tried not to show her horror as they walked. The rugs were faded, no doubt the floorboards they covered were discolored as a result, and the crown molding was cracked where it met the ceiling.

"I used to spend my summers here, growing up," Chris said. "I don't remember it being in such bad shape then. I guess the last few years were difficult." His eyes took on a hard look as he stared out the window, and she was starting to wonder if he wasn't thinking about the condition of the house anymore.

"Do you have cleaning crews coming?" She had a bad feeling that because she even had to ask this, the answer would be that he did not.

He tossed up his hands. "I'm told that their first available appointment is two weeks out."

"But the estate sale is this weekend," she said aloud. She chewed her thumbnail, then, remembering her manicure, dropped it.

"Thanks for the reminder," he said, an edge to his tone. He looked around the room they were standing in now, one of the rooms that had a pile of tarps in the corner. Had he just planned to leave them there, in a dusty heap?

He looked lost, like a little boy who was told to clean his room and didn't know where to start. Sarah believed that if he had a bed to stuff everything under right now, he would do just that. And maybe he had. She hadn't been upstairs yet.

To think there was another full floor of this house! She fought back a growing sense of panic.

This was for Hannah. And for her job.

"Well, I guess we'd better get started then," she said, pulling in a shaky breath. When she'd offered to help, she hadn't realized just how bad of shape things were in. She'd been so set on her mission to sell her idea to him yesterday that she'd sort of glazed over the details of the house when she'd walked through it. Now she realized that he needed her help. Needed it badly.

And if this was what it took to get on good terms with her boss and give a friend the wedding of her dreams, then so be it.

"Well, why don't you tell me what you've done so far and what we still have to do?"

She looked at him, waiting for a response, but he just gave her a bewildered shrug and said, "I've been pulling off tarps—"

"I see that." Her eyes widened on the pile of them. "Do you have a dumpster we could take them to?"

"I missed the trash pickup," he admitted sheepishly. "I wouldn't have been ready in time anyway. I have a bulk pickup scheduled for this Friday."

Well, that was something. Not much, but better than nothing.

"I've been dusting. Sorting through drawers. Cleaning out closets."

Some progress then. And if they worked together, they could get things dusted and polished in time for Saturday. Still, this place had the potential to be something better. Something truly beautiful. And she wanted to help restore it to what it once was and could still be.

"And for the estate sale," she said, trying not to allow herself to become as overwhelmed as Chris clearly was when her eyes homed in on a curio cabinet full of figurines, wall after wall of paintings, and tables full of vases and statues. "Do you plan to put everything out?"

"Jeff McDowell suggested that the place would show better if it was cleared out a bit. Hence the reason for the sale. But I still think there's too much here. Not everything will sell."

She didn't want to break it to him that he'd be lucky if a third of it sold. It was a home that had been passed down through the generations, and collections had been added to it over time.

"I think it would help if we took down some of the drapery. They're difficult to clean and probably add to the dust. It would let more light in too." She eyed the thick, velvet panels that seemed to flank each window and darkened the rooms. While pretty, they were a sign of their times, and buyers would want to freshen the place up a bit. That would be a quick fix, something they could knock off their list in less than an hour, with any luck.

If they got past the missing shingles on the roof and the windows which were clearly original and probably did a poor job, if any, at insulation.

He nodded. "Good idea. I can take those down with a ladder. Someone might want to buy them?" He cut her a glance but the quick shake of her head shut down that idea right away.

"I'm happy to help sort things into piles for you. That way when the truck comes on Friday we can discard anything that you won't keep or plan to sell."

"There's nothing I want to keep," he said in a clipped tone, sharp enough to pull her attention away from the cobwebs that seemed to be climbing the ornate drapes that were also fading at the folds. Yes, they had to go.

"Nothing?" She frowned at him. Not a picture or a clock or that stunning grand piano she'd noticed in the front room?

"Nothing," he said crisply and turned away before she could say anything more. He picked up the pile of tarps. "I'll bring these out to the garage. We may as well store everything out there until Friday so it's out of the way."

"Good idea," she said. "I know you said you were going room by room, but the dust and cobwebs won't clean themselves. Let's pull the tarps from each room, clean, then decide what's worth trying to sell and what isn't."

He stared at her for a long moment, his expression unreadable. "Fair enough. Bottom to top or top to bottom?"

She wasn't sure it mattered, but because she was eager to see the rest of the house, she said, "Top to bottom."

"There's an attic," Chris said. "The stairs go all the way up to the third floor. Most of the stuff in there is old junk, but if you see something that looks worth putting out for the sale, we can bring it downstairs and find a home for it."

She stood in the room while he carried the tarps down a hall. A moment later she heard a door banging, and some fresh air filtered through the dust. She sneezed. Three times in a row. Her nose was itching and her eyes were watering and she started to wonder what would happen if they didn't get the place fixed up in time. Would he still let them hold the wedding here? Abby would need to use the kitchen for her catering and food prep. Did the oven even work, let alone the fridge? Would Hannah even want her wedding here if she saw the condition of the place close up?

She started to honestly wonder just what Chloe would even say once she stepped inside, until Sarah looked out the window, onto the wide stone terrace that overlooked the garden bursting with petals of all sizes and colors, and her resolve strengthened. A stone bench sat under a weeping willow. The waves rolled in the sea just beyond the lawn.

She could do this. She had to do this. So what if she'd probably get hives from all this dust?

Tomorrow she wouldn't wear any mascara. It was just dripping down her cheeks, no doubt. It's not like she had to impress the man.

Still, as she watched his muscles strain against his light blue tee shirt as he carried the tarps to the carriage house at the far side of the house, she felt a strange flicker of excitement. One she promptly put in check.

Right. The attic. Maybe it would be less dusty.

She nearly laughed out loud at that. She'd always had too much hope for her own good. But not anymore. Now she was going to be practical. Lower her expectations. But she wouldn't be a cynic. She couldn't be a cynic. Not if she wanted to keep her job at Bayside Brides.

She walked back into the front hallway and started her ascent up the wide, bridal staircase, that seemed to swirl three levels above her and likely did. This house was huge, full of antiques, but more than that, it was full of memories.

Memories that seemed to mean as little to Chris as the house itself did.

Or perhaps, instead of not meaning anything, they meant too much.

Her hand grazed the banister as she moved toward the top of the house, pausing only slightly at the landing on the second floor, where hallways spread in both directions, interrupted only by rows of closed doors. She'd heard the house had nine bedrooms, but the downstairs was even larger, with a conservatory, library, and dining room that could seat twenty-four.

What kind of family would buy this house, she wondered, as she moved up the last few steps that stopped short just outside a single closed door. She opened the door to a dark space and fumbled her hand along the wall for a light switch, hoping it wouldn't find a spider instead.

Luckily, the switch was found quickly, and it was functioning. All at once, the room sprang to life before her, and she scanned her eyes, taking it all in. It must have been over a hundred degrees in there. There were two windows in the room, at either end of the space, but both were dusty and in need of a cleaning, letting in a sad, murky hint of sunlight and, she guessed, there was next to no chance they would open and let in some fresh air. She was already beginning to sweat (ever so attractive), and she wiped her forehead with the back of her hand. Her palms felt grimy.

There were suitcases and trunks and paintings stacked against a wall. And boxes, piled at random, most of them not labeled, she noticed with a frown.

She suddenly missed Bayside Brides more than ever. The cool, calm storefront, with the lovely bouquets of flowers and the gorgeous, frothy material at every turn. The jewelry sparkling in its case. The classical music that played ever so softly in the distance.

She felt wretched. Hot, sweaty, already eager for a shower.

Best to get it over with. Eye on the prize and all that.

She started with the paintings, wondering if she might stumble upon something of value, but there was nothing that her untrained eye could see. A few seascapes, probably painted by a local artist at some point. Still, she set them to the side. They'd do well at the estate sale. People were always eager to buy up any kind of history when it came to Oyster Bay.

Well, except for the dilapidated mansion. Still, she'd be sure to mention these paintings to Dottie Joyce, who was the head of the Historical Society. She was nearly certain that Dottie would have a personal desire for at least one of them and a professional interest in a couple of others.

Next she moved on to suitcases, which were empty and of no real value judging by the loose handles and frayed corners. She set those in a pile of things that could be discarded—with Chris's approval, of course. It seemed odd that he would let a relative stranger go through these items, but then, she supposed they didn't belong to him at all, only in the legal sense. Perhaps he was just as detached from them all as she was. And with the scale of the house, he needed all the help he could get.

Really, she was doing him a huge favor. Meaning she deserved one in return.

The real project in the room was the stacks of trunks and the boxes. She spent the better part of half an hour going through the first box, which mostly seemed to be clothes, men's clothes, all of which eventually went into the discard pile. The next box was more rewarding: a vintage train set that she was certain the owners of the antique shop would pay a premium for. This she kept in the box. She'd ask Chris if it still worked, later. If he even knew.

She combed through a few more boxes, sneezing as she went, all too aware that by now her nose and eyes were both running and that her hair was frizzing into wisps around her face. Soon, she'd take a break, just for some air. Or water.

Not to check in on Chris. Nope.

But first... She paused. Now this was interesting. Photos, an entire chest of them. She couldn't imagine how these would go in the discard or sale piles. Surely these were too personal for even Chris to part with? She sorted through a few, smiling as she went. Many were black and white, others faded photos, most captured here in this very house, or out in the back, near the water. They were of Marty, as a younger man, and some had other people featured in them. A woman reappeared. Marty's wife, she assumed.

She set the photos back in the box, carefully, and picked up an album, expecting it to reveal page after page of equally old photos, maybe even wedding photos from Marty's big day. but these were in color, glossy, and there was Chris. With a woman. A very pretty woman. They were sitting on chairs, on the beach, and she was laughing. She had light brown hair and tanned skin, long legs jetting out from a sleek, black, one-piece bathing suit. And Chris was looking at her, smiling, leaning back with a drink in his hand, without a care in the world.

She stared at the picture, trying to figure out when this would have been taken. There was no date stamp on the back. And nothing else in the album revealed anything more. It was recent. A few years ago, maybe. Chris seemed so happy. So content. She wondered who the woman was, and if she was still in his life.

And no, she was not jealous. Or disappointed. Nope. Not going there anymore.

She hadn't even heard Chris come in until he spoke. "Find anything interesting?"

She jumped, closed the book with a slap, and turned guiltily to face him as she stood up. "There's an entire trunk of old photographs here."

He frowned but stepped forward, studying the open crate as he approached. "Toss it all."

"But...there are some of your uncle in here." She reached down to grab a few, holding them out to Chris.

He heaved a sigh, running a hand through his hair. "Set those aside then. I'll sort through them later."

Well, at least he was being reasonable. "There's one of you in here, too." She picked up the album again, opening it to the first page.

Immediately, Chris's expression hardened. "I changed my mind. There's no reason to hold onto dusty old photographs."

"None of them?" She stared at him, aghast. "But these are priceless! They're...they're memories. They can never be replaced."

"Exactly." His jaw was set, his eyes stony. "Everything in this house can go. What can't sell at the sale will be hauled away next week."

He took the album from her hand and set it back in the trunk. He pulled the lid. It slammed shut, making her jump. "This was a mistake," he said, shaking his head. "I just need to sell this house, not invest any more time into it."

"But—" She blinked, trying to understand what had just happened, what she'd done wrong.

"I'm sorry," he said, backing away toward the staircase. "This was a mistake." He looked around the room, seeming almost pained. "This was all a mistake."

Eight

Chris had just finished bringing down the last of the items from the attic when the doorbell rang. He set the painting in his hand against a wall and walked into the hallway, his speed picking up when he considered that it might be Sarah—back again—and he realized that he almost hoped it was her. God knew he needed the help. Besides, he felt bad. And he felt bad enough as it was lately.

He'd overreacted, taken his frustration out on the nearest person, and pushed back against a situation that she hadn't created and that couldn't go away.

None of it would go away. Not until this house was sold. Not until he closed the door on it for a final time.

He'd apologize. Tell Sarah that he'd been wrong. And he had been wrong. It wasn't Sarah he was mad at. It was this house. The memories it stirred up.

He opened the door, eager to get it out there, to have the air cleared as well as his conscience, but it wasn't

Sarah on the front stoop. It was another woman, a woman he didn't recognize. A pretty woman with dark hair and a big smile.

"Are you Chris Foster?" she asked, tilting her head.

He nodded, guarded. "I am." He had an instinct to close the door, and he inched it forward. Back in Boston, no one showed up at his door uninvited except salespeople. People wanting something. And he didn't want anything right now other than to be left alone.

Except that the past few hours since he'd sent Sarah away, he realized that maybe that wasn't what he'd wanted after all. The house felt huge and quiet. When Sarah was here he wasn't haunted by the ghosts. He wasn't focused on the past. He was present. Normally only work could do that for him. Here he didn't even have that escape.

"I'm Hannah Donovan. The photographer? Jim McDowell asked me to take some photos for the real estate listing."

"Of course." He felt foolish as he extended a hand to her. He didn't know what he'd been expecting. He'd grown too used to being alone in recent years, to limiting human interaction to what he wanted, to keeping life on his terms. In his control. "Come on inside." He stepped back, letting her pass, watching as her eyes rose to the ceiling, the oversized, ornate chandelier that he had cleaned yesterday with an extension pole, a ladder, and a silent prayer. Her mouth dropped slightly.

"This is gorgeous!" She immediately began snapping

some photos of the staircase with the camera she pulled from her canvas bag.

"Do you work for the real estate office?" he asked. His tee shirt clung to him and he felt the need to apologize for the heat. He could only hope that the weather would be kind to him this weekend.

She glanced over her shoulder. "Oh, no. I work for the newspaper, actually, but I do freelance work on the side. There aren't many photographers in a town this small, as you can imagine."

There wasn't much of anything in a town this small, not that he particularly minded. It was still a beautiful town with a rocky shoreline and a town center full of one-of-a-kind shops: an ice cream parlor, a few restaurants, a book store, candy shop. Life was simpler here. Easier. Or it should have been...

"This is actually my lunch break, so I won't take long," she said.

He glanced at his watch. It was already after one, and he hadn't stopped to eat. He hadn't thought to buy any food, and he hated to go into town and waste time. He'd keep going. Push through until the sun went down. Then he'd go back to the hotel and order room service. Shower first.

"Take as long as you'd like," he heard himself saying. He frowned at that. Since when did he long for company? He hadn't yearned for so much as a pet fish back in Boston. He was content with his work, his television, and his favorite take-out delivery spots.

Maybe not quite content. But he was getting by.

"Well, don't mind me," Hannah said as she wandered into the dining room and snapped a few more photographs of the built-in cabinets and the tall, arched, shaped windows that offset the otherwise deep red walls. "I'll go through each room and then take a few of the backyard."

"It's a bit of a mess," Chris rushed to explain as he followed her into the front parlor, where another pile of tarps was lying on the floor. "I'm in the process of getting it ready."

"It's okay," she said, brushing off his concern. "I can tweak these a bit on my computer before I send them to Jim. I've always admired this house, actually, so it's a real treat to finally see the inside."

"Oh?" He felt a displaced sense of flattery at the comment. After all, it wasn't his home. Legally it was, but nothing beyond that.

Still, it was his family's home. He'd taken it for granted, all those summers here. Jenna had loved the house, and he'd tried to see the beauty through her eyes, but he was too close to it. Sometimes it was only once you'd taken a step back that you could appreciate what you once had.

He swallowed hard. No thinking of any of that now.

"My sister and I used to ride our bikes over here as kids and try to get a closer look at it. I remember one time the garden was featured in a newspaper article and I saved the clippings." Her cheeks turned a little pink as she held the camera at her chest. "Sorry. That must make me sound like a bit of a creep."

"More like a potential buyer," he said, rolling back on his heels.

"Ha!" She snapped a picture of the grand piano in the corner of the room. "I wish." She took another photo, and then another, before turning back to him. "But someone who can afford this will come along, I'm sure. I mean, who wouldn't love a house like this?"

She grinned, and then, widening her eyes for his permission, let herself into the adjacent library.

Chris held back, staring at the piano, remembering his uncle sitting on the bench, playing something melancholy but equally beautiful. Chris never knew the name and had never heard it again. Now he wished he'd thought to ask what it was, just to hear it one last time.

There were a lot of things he would have done differently if he'd known it would be his last chance.

He could hear the camera clicking, over and over. Suddenly, the thought of selling the house felt all too real. It was one thing to have an estate sale, to get rid of the faded furniture, to clear out rooms that probably hadn't been used in decades. Marty only used a portion of the house. Kept the rest shut off. Said the electric bill would have been sky-high otherwise.

Now, though, there was a photographer. Someone capturing each room from different angles. And there was Jim, who would post these photos online, probably today, for the world to see. For the world to judge. For the world to decide if they wanted to buy it. Own it.

It was the reality of the situation, he told himself. It was no different than when he'd listed the house he lived in with Jenna, and watched as they photographed rooms that she'd decorated. The fake plant in the corner of the living room behind the beige sofa. The colorful area rug that had been a wedding gift from her parents. The over-sized clock on the wall near the kitchen table that had ticked away their time together, without him even knowing.

He walked into the library, painted a handsome hunter green, with dark furniture which Hannah was saying would "show well." The books that lined the shelves might sell to a collector. If not, he would donate them to the Oyster Bay Library, in Marty's name. Most of them were classics, some were history books. Marty had always been a reader.

Now, as someone who lived alone himself, he longed to have one last conversation with Marty. To ask how he did it. How he kept from going crazy. How he busied himself on those lonely winter nights when the wind was howling and the snow was coming down and all that he had to fill the silence were the memories that couldn't be banished, no matter how hard he tried.

The house grew quiet as Hannah moved through it, first the day room, the kitchen, the various little pockets on the first floor, and then upstairs, while he waited below, staring at the piles of tarps in the corners. Each one he removed seemed to bring the house further back to life. Back to the way it used to be.

Finally, she came downstairs, grinning broadly, and he led her through the halls into the conservatory, which gave a view of the back terrace and the grounds beyond it. He stayed inside, watching as she snapped photos of the carriage house and the extensive garden.

Eventually, he opened one of the French doors and stepped outside. The temperature outside was hot, but not as hot as the air inside of the house. Hannah caught his eye and waved.

"Almost done here," she said as she snapped a few more shots of the back of the house. "The ivy growing up the stone really adds a special touch. It's a stunning property."

It was, he knew it was, but he couldn't be so objective about it, and that was just the problem.

"I have a confession to make actually," she said, letting the camera drop back against her chest from the strap that hung around her neck. "I always dreamed of getting married here. Right here, actually. In this very spot."

She smiled and stood facing the garden, where roses seemed to burst with every color. "Wouldn't this be the most beautiful place to have a wedding? With this stone backdrop and the terrace expanding to the gardens and the sea?"

He swallowed hard, hoping the tension didn't show in his face. This photographer was a nice woman, a happy one, too, and from the ring that sparkled on her finger, she had weddings on the brain.

She didn't need to know how his had turned out. She didn't need to know that it wasn't all sunshine and roses.

"It would be a beautiful place to have a wedding," he said sadly, his eyes pained as he took in the view and then looked back up at the great stone house towering above him.

And it had been.

At six that evening, Sarah pulled her car to a stop in the lot outside of Serenity Hills and sank her face into her hands. She had blown it. Not just the chance to have Hannah's wedding day saved, but also the chance to save her career. And the worst part of all was that she didn't even know what she had done wrong!

She'd replayed the events from this morning all day, and still, she couldn't make sense of it. But it didn't matter if she understood or not, she supposed. Chris had made his decision, just like Chloe had made hers. She'd messed up. And now…Well, now she would do what she always did every Wednesday evening and visit her grandmother.

And then she would go home and put together a resume. Forget finding a man when she had to find a new job! She'd ask around, see if Posy needed a second hand at the flower shop. She wouldn't mind making arrangements.

Even if they would be for weddings that Chloe would be planning.

She groaned, grabbed the white bakery box from Angie's, and pushed open her car door. No time for pity now. For the next hour, she had to shelve it. But she highly doubted she'd succeed in forgetting about it.

There was once a time when she could see her grandmother looking out the front window at her, anticipating
her arrival in a blue wingback chair that gave her good
posture, something ladies of her generation prided themselves on, she would remark, in a passive-aggressive way
of hers that Sarah had come to find charming. She carried
the box of chocolate chip cookies with her, but her heart
still sank a little when she entered the lobby and saw that
no one was in the window, even though she had called
ahead to let her grandmother know she would be stopping by that day. Esther had no other grandchildren, and
Sarah's parents didn't get to town to visit as much as she
knew her father would have liked.

Lately, her grandmother perked up when Sarah told
the stories from Bayside Brides. Esther especially liked the
part when someone pitched a fit, like the bride who
ripped a veil from her head so hard that Sarah could have
sworn a bit of hair came out with it, all because her
mother and she disagreed over the length for twenty-five
minutes while Chloe nodded and murmured soothing
words, and Melanie had to keep excusing herself to the
storage room to have a good hard laugh. Today, though,
the only titillating story Sarah would be able to share was
her own personal conflict, and she didn't want to dwell
on it.

She found her grandmother in the courtyard, sitting
on a bench near the hydrangea bushes. It was a warm
evening, but not hot enough to melt the chocolate chips
in the cookies, and Sarah proffered the box as she took a
seat beside her.

"How was your date?" her grandmother said in response, and despite the reminder of last Friday's disappointment, Sarah was pleased to hear it. It meant her grandmother remembered their last conversation, and that today's visit would hopefully be a good one.

"Oh...he had to cancel."

"*Had* to?" Esther's mouth pinched. "Pity. A pretty, young girl like you should be turning heads. What's wrong with these men nowadays?"

"Tell me about it," Sarah grumbled, but the truth of the matter was that the person she was starting to wonder about was herself. After all, every day at work she met women who had not only succeeded in finding a boyfriend, but a man who wanted to commit. She couldn't even have a guy stick to a date with her anymore.

Maybe Melanie was right. She was looking in the wrong places. Falling for the wrong types. She was setting herself up to fail.

But Melanie wasn't right about Chris.

"Well, the men here at Serenity aren't much better," Esther said as she pulled out a chocolate chip cookie and took a small bite. "A couple of ladies thought it might be a good idea to have a dance every Saturday. Do you know how many men came to the event last weekend?"

Sarah tried to estimate how many men must live at the home who would even be capable of walking, much less dancing. "I don't know. Twenty?"

"Try two." Esther's eyes narrowed. "And one was

Earl. He doesn't count. He was only there because his blushing bride got her hair done specially for it."

Of course, Earl was married to Mimi Harper, who was Bridget, Margo, and Abby's grandmother. It was her second wedding, and a fairly recent one, but a blushing bride? Sarah couldn't help but laugh.

"It isn't funny. Just because you get to be my age doesn't mean you have to give up hope."

Sarah looked at her grandmother, properly. "No, I suppose it doesn't." Still, she'd never thought of it that way, and truth be told, she'd gone and given it up herself, hadn't she?

If her grandmother could still believe that she might find love again, then who was Sarah to think she couldn't?

Buoyed by this newfound belief that everything might just work out, and for the both of them, she took a cookie from the box. But her grandmother slapped her hand. Hard enough to sting.

"Ouch!" Sarah stared at her.

"Don't go ruining that pretty figure of yours. I intend to attend your wedding before I croak."

"Grandma." Sarah shook her head, but the truth was that her grandmother's comment hurt. Badly. She wanted her grandmother to come to her wedding someday. She'd seen so many brides come through the shop whose eyes shone with tears over the people who had been lost, who wouldn't be there on their special day. With Esther's health declining, she wanted to savor every moment she had, to make the most of each day.

"And you'll wear my pearls," Esther was saying. The certainty in her voice told Sarah that she must have already planned this all out, and Sarah felt sad to disappoint her, even though she'd already planned to have her friend Beth design one of her custom jewelry sets that she now sold on consignment at Bayside Brides. "It's a family tradition."

"That's nice to think about," Sarah said wistfully. She'd already picked out her dress. Well, the truth was that she'd already picked out about a hundred dresses. She had always wanted to be ready when the day came, and know all her options. But more and more there were too many options and not enough reason to even consider them.

"I have a whole box set aside of things that I want you to have," Esther said. She looked at Sarah earnestly. "You promise me, right?"

Sarah set a hand down on her grandmother's wrist. It felt thinner than it had been just a few short weeks ago. "Of course," she said softly. "I'll treasure them."

They fell into silence while Esther ate her cookie, slowly, savoring each bite. The other five in the box might be shared with the staff (if they were in Esther's good graces, which wasn't often the case) or Mimi and Earl, more likely.

She'd never thought about what Esther might leave her. She'd assumed that everything would go to her parents, and the fact that her grandmother had been thoughtful enough to set something aside touched her in a bittersweet way. It made her want to hold on to the woman beside her a little tighter, even as she slowly slipped away.

"Grandma, did you ever see Marty Foster when he was here?" she asked. Chris had mentioned that his uncle was here in the last few years of his life. It wasn't a big place. Surely his path would have crossed with Esther's at some point. Considering that her grandmother had crushed on everyone from ninety-four-year-old Mitch LaMore to a thirty-ish male nurse, she was surprised she hadn't heard anything about Marty before.

"Did I ever see him?" she quipped. "Had lunch with him a few times in the cafeteria. Tried to see if he might be interested in a little *bingo* one night, but he made it clear that he was not. Shame." She tutted and looked out in the garden.

Sarah decided not to ask if *bingo* was code for something she didn't need to visualize. "What was he like?"

"Oh, handsome." Her grandmother smiled.

Like Chris, Sarah thought.

"He was younger than me, but not by much. It wouldn't have been scandalous or anything if...Well. Marty made it very clear to every woman here that he was devoted to one person and one person only. Widower, you know."

Sarah knew she should not be thinking of Chris right now, but she couldn't help it, not because he was cute or anything, but because he had asked her to leave, and she couldn't understand why.

"Did he ever have any visitors?" Sarah asked.

Esther thought about it and then shook her head.

"They never had children. She had an accident on a horse, as I recall. She loved riding. Lots of women had an interest in him for a while. He broke many a heart."

"How tragic," Sarah said.

"You can say that again. A handsome man like that. Rich, too." Esther slid her a glance as she waggled her eyebrows and Sarah barked out a laugh.

"I meant that it was tragic he never got over it," Sarah said.

"Lived in that great big house all alone," Esther tutted. "Had a falling out with his younger brother. No other siblings. There was a nephew, though. Marty talked about him every chance he had."

At the mention of Chris, Sarah bristled. She reached for a cookie, and then, catching Esther's eye, snatched her hand back. Good thing there was a tub of mint-choco-late-chip ice cream waiting in her freezer at home.

"Did you ever go to the house? Crestview Manor?" Sarah asked, eager to shift the topic away from Chris but not completely off the subject of the Foster estate. Maybe there was another way. Another person she could talk to who was connected to the house and who might have some influence on whether they would allow the property to be rented for a night. Esther had lived in town before moving into Serenity Hills. Perhaps she knew more than she was letting on.

"No, can't say that I was ever there. But a few people in town were invited to the wedding a few years back."

"Wedding?"

"The nephew's wedding," Esther said, but Sarah

could barely hear her, her blood was rushing in her ears. "Heard it was quite an elaborate event. A big brass band and everything. You could hear the music three miles down the shoreline."

A wedding. But Chris had been adamant that he wasn't the marrying kind. That he wasn't looking to settle down or have a family.

Bad divorce, she thought, feeling the weight of disappointment. He'd been burned, and he clearly wasn't over it if the reaction to the photos said anything. And while once a broken heart might have been something she'd think they had in common, something to say, latch on to, now she just took it for what it was. The man wasn't looking to remarry. And she wasn't looking for a man anymore, especially the wrong kind of man.

But she was looking to keep her job, and Chris was the only one who had the power to help her.

She'd just have to find a way to help him again. And now that she understood where she'd gone wrong today, she might just have a chance to fix it.

Nine

It took Sarah two hours to work up the nerve to finally leave her apartment the next morning. Another cup of coffee was always a good stall tactic. Finally, because she knew with certainty what would happen if she didn't try with Chris again, but she had no way of knowing what would happen if she did try, she climbed onto her bike and pedaled up the shoreline to Crestview Manor, dread twisting her gut.

The gate was open when she arrived, and from the base of the drive, she could see Chris in the open doorway, in a tee shirt and jeans. He appeared to be sanding something.

He'd bought sandpaper. Somehow this amused her.

He stopped working when he heard her bicycle crunching over the gravel and she mustered up a friendly wave. See, nothing strange here. Just popping by the place she had been told to leave, for basically the second time. Stalkerish? Hardly. Just doing her community service.

Just holding up her end of the bargain.

"You're back," was all he said, his tone mild, if not slightly amused.

A good thing? She hoped so.

She kicked out the stand to her bike, made sure it was secure, and took a long, shaky breath, before walking up the long, flagstone path, shoving her hands into the pockets of her jean shorts.

She could always say she had lost something here. An earring, perhaps? But that would be lame. And she wasn't the kind of girl who made up excuses to see a guy—not anymore. Besides, there was nothing to be nervous about in this case, well, other than the obvious possibility of outright banishment, a call to the cops, or a threat of a restraining order, all of which would be a tad embarrassing but something she'd learn to accept in her professional life as of late.

"I wanted to apologize," she said instead. Treat him as you would a client, she'd told herself the entire bike ride over, plus those two extra hours spent pacing her apartment. She had overstepped, upset him, however inadvertently, and she should make amends. She'd consider it practice for her meeting with Chloe on Monday.

"No, I'm the one who should apologize," he said, surprising her. He looked up, swearing under his breath as he waved his hand in front of his face. "Damn bees. Here, come inside. Please."

She tried to keep her expression neutral, but she might have done a fist pump when he turned his back. He was letting her in. He was sorry. One crisis in her life was finally averted.

She followed him inside, careful to keep her tone calm, her smile serene. But one look at the scrubbed mirror and the shining light fixtures made her self-control go wayside, and she dropped her jaw dramatically. "Wow! You've been busy in my absence!"

"Well, I didn't think you would come back," he said, giving her a sheepish smile.

"Please," she said, grinning broadly now. "I think you've learned by now that I don't back down that easily."

"No, and to be honest, I'm happy that you don't." He smiled, but there was an intensity in his dark eyes that made Sarah's breath catch.

It wasn't her that he had missed. It had been the help. The extra set of hands.

She turned away, trying to think of something witty to say to break the sudden tension. "Of course, there is the fact that while I'm stubborn you seem to have a bit of a temper."

"Actually, I'm one of the most carefree people you'll ever meet," he said, raising a hand as if he were taking an oath.

She didn't know whether to believe him or not. "So you're not going to kick me out again?"

"I'm a man of my word," he said, setting the same hand to his chest. The sincerity of his gesture touched her, but then she thought of what her grandmother had revealed and decided that she couldn't afford to let anything about this man touch her. If he was a man of his word then he meant what he said when he told her that he wasn't ever looking to get married.

And the truth of the matter was that she was hoping to get married someday. She wanted the white picket fence, the kids, the family dinners, and holiday traditions. She couldn't help it. She just wasn't holding out for it anymore.

"In fact, as a peace offering, let me make it up to you." He took a step forward. She saw that he had dust in his hair. His eyes were a bit bloodshot, and she noticed that he was wearing the same shirt as yesterday. Had he spent the whole night here?

Probably. And damn if she didn't feel a little sorry for the guy for that.

"A peace offering." She bit her lip. Just what could he be offering? A small figurine from the curio cabinet? The conservatory for the cocktail reception (Hannah and Chloe would both swoon over that coop!)?

"Lunch," he said simply.

She gave him a hard look. "Lunch?"

It's not a date, it's not a date, it's not a date.

"Well, if you call sandwiches and sodas I picked up in town with my breakfast this morning lunch."

"I do call that lunch," she said, trying not to smile.

It's not a date, Sarah.

"Okay, then." He blew out a breath and looked around the rooms that jetted out on every side. He seemed nearly as relieved as he did bewildered. "Maybe we can tackle some of the bedrooms and work up an appetite?"

"Lead the way," she said. And no, she did not check out his broad shoulders as she followed him down the hall.

Well, maybe just a little.

They climbed the stairs, single file, and this time, she kept her eyes trained on the floor. Hardwood. A bit of fading. Otherwise good condition. They approached the landing, which she'd only passed yesterday, and Chris reached to open the first door on the left. It was a bedroom. Bright, despite the heavy teal-blue curtains that hung from the window, with simple furnishings: a small white desk in the corner, with an upholstered chair in blue and pink. A double bed with a simple pink cover-let. The walls were decorated with seascapes, similar to the ones she'd seen in the attic. She wanted to ask who painted them, but she didn't want to stir up any memory of yesterday. Today was a fresh start.

She walked to the nearest window and pulled back the curtains. All at once the room filled with more light and a stunning view of the sea. "I like the use of blue in this room. It feels...beachy."

She glanced at Chris, but he shrugged. She assumed that decorating wasn't his thing, which was why it was good that she was here to help!

She walked to the second window and reached for the curtains, but there was a rustling at the bottom of the fabric, where it met the floor, and before she could even process what was happening, a tiny grey mouse dashed out from under the drapery and scooted behind the desk. A sound filled the room. Shrill, loud. Petrified.

Dear God, it was coming from her mouth.

When she clamped it shut, she realized her entire body was shaking, and she stared wide-eyed at Chris, whose hand was covering his mouth, his face red as his shoulders shook nearly as hard as her own.

Only he wasn't shaking from fear. He was shaking from amusement.

"It's a mouse!" she cried, pointing in the direction of the desk. "Didn't you see it?"

"Oh, I saw it, all right." Chris struggled to compose himself. He pushed his hair back off his forehead, taking in a breath that did little to pull the smile from his face. "God, I needed that," he said under his breath, and then he started chuckling again.

Now, she was mad. Really mad. She put her hands on her hips and gave him a stony stare. "Well, I didn't. That thing came out of nowhere! I could have been bit."

"Mice don't bite."

She raised an eyebrow. "You sure?"

His pause told her that he wasn't sure, and so, muttering something she couldn't quite hear, he crossed the room to the window where she now stood, and opened the French door leading out to the balcony.

Sarah frowned. "If you send it out there, how will it get to the ground?"

He glanced over his shoulder. "Now you're suddenly concerned about its welfare?"

"Fine," she said, shuddering at the idea of being alone in the room with the mouse. Or worse, having it get loose somewhere in the house.

With that in mind, she walked to the door to the hallway and quickly shut it, just in time to watch Chris inch the desk away from the wall and peer over the edge. Her body went stiff with tension. She barely breathed as she watched. Wanted to jump up on something, but the nearest chair was by the desk.

"I don't see it," he finally said. "I think it's gone."

"Gone?" Sarah felt the blood drain from her face. She edged toward him, her heart racing, and then—

There was the sound again. Louder than last time. A scream so shrill she was almost impressed by the power of her pitch. And oh no, she was clinging to him. His back. Her fingers clawing at his tee shirt. She could feel the cotton, smooth on her fingertips, a strange opposition to the heat radiating off his skin. He was strong. Thick. And...

And he was laughing at her.

Tears filled his eyes as he sputtered and shook, and this time she knew it wasn't from the dust. For one fleeting moment, she forgot all about the rodent and struggled not to take a good, hard swat at him. But then she remembered. Her entire body went stiff. And oh...oh...

She jumped on the chair.

"It can probably climb up there," he said, still laughing so hard that he struggled to get the words out.

"Are you kidding me?" she all but shouted. "Get it out! Get it out!"

"Get a broom," he said, clutching his side.

She considered her options. To open the door risked letting the thing have free roam of the house. But to not...

She jumped off the chair and, as fast as she could, darted to the door and slipped out. She stood, panting, and then ran down the stairs. She found the broom in the kitchen, with a box of other cleaning supplies, and brought it up the stairs, this time not risking going in. Instead, she knocked. Chris opened the door wide enough to reach out his hand, and she placed the broom inside it.

A few minutes later he emerged, doing a sorry job of trying to look somber.

By then, she had composed herself. Had even started to worry he might send her home again, tell her she was no help if she was scared of a mouse.

But he just cut her a glance and then burst out laughing again.

"Well, at least that's over," she said, lifting her chin a notch. But Chris just raised an eyebrow, his expression knowing, and she frowned at him. Deeply.

"I think I'll start on the next bedroom," she said and walked to the other side of the hall, just in case. Honestly, she thought as she entered the room, this one done up in green and pink, if Chloe even dared to say she hadn't shown how desperately she wanted to keep her job at

Bayside Brides after this, then there was truly nothing more she could say.

She glanced at the clock on the bedside table after gingerly checking under the drapes for any more surprises. How many more hours until lunch?

"So I have to ask," Sarah said as she took a spot beside Chris on the shore and untied her gym shoes. She wiggled her toes into the sand, happy to have some fresh air on her face. They were making progress on the house, but they still had a long way to go, and truth be told, she was exhausted. She'd spent the better part of the morning helping Chris beat the rugs. They'd considered getting rid of them until they saw how much darker the floorboards were under them. "Did you have lunch plans with someone else?"

He frowned as he handed her a sandwich wrapped in the waxy paper that Angie's was known for. "I don't know anyone else in this town. Why do you ask?"

"Well, you have two sandwiches here," she pointed out.

He laughed. "I planned ahead. Figured I'd be stuck here for dinner, too."

The man had given her his dinner. If that wasn't a romantic gesture, she didn't know what was.

Except it wasn't romantic, she told herself firmly. He was just apologizing to her the best way he knew how. He was being...nice, she realized.

She smiled to herself. Nice was good.

"You just might be stuck here for dinner with the amount of work we still have left to do." She unwrapped the paper to discover a turkey sandwich underneath. She took a hearty bite, nearly groaning at the taste. "Sorry," she said, sliding him a glance. "I'm not used to so much physical exertion this early in the day."

And she wasn't used to cramming a sandwich into her mouth in as big of bites as she could physically handle, especially not in front of a decent-looking guy. More than decent. But then, this one wasn't an option. Made things very straightforward from the get-go.

She wiped the crumbs from her mouth with the back of her hand, wondering if Chris was looking at her in astonishment. But considering that he was doing the same, he probably could have eaten both of these sandwiches for his lunch. Heck, she probably could have.

"So you spent all these summers here and you never got to know anyone?" she asked.

He shrugged. "I stayed around the house mostly. Fishing. Playing in the yard. There was plenty to do."

"No brothers or sisters?"

"Only child," he said with a twinge of regret in his tone.

She gave him a little smile. "Me too. I don't mind it so much. Except when my parents get a little too curious about my personal life. That's why I decided to move here. I've been here for over a year now. It suits me. I've made a lot of really good friends and, well, they feel like family. Plus, my grandmother's here, but I think I mentioned that."

And she was rambling. She tended to do this when she was nervous, or there was a potential for silence, or, in this case, she didn't exactly trust herself not to mess up and accidentally stir up the wife again. She needed to beat some rugs. Dust some sconces. Keep her head low.

Mentioning her grandmother made her think of the conversation with Esther last night. The music from the band could be heard three miles down the shoreline, she'd said. What a wedding that must have been.

"I used to wish my parents would take an interest in my personal life." Chris gave her a little grin that made her heart speed up.

For no good reason, she reminded herself.

"They shipped me off to boarding school as a kid. I spent my summers here. In some ways, I was closer to Marty than I've ever been to my father."

"You must miss him," she said, hoping that she wasn't hedging into dangerous territory, but he just gave a little shrug and smiled out over the water.

"I do. I wish I had visited more in the past few years but, well, life got busy." He peeled off more of the wax paper and took a big bite of his sandwich. "Work," he clarified after he'd swallowed.

"Which is?"

"I'm a financial planner. Which is part of the reason I know what a money pit an estate like this is," he added wryly.

Sarah took a smaller bite this time, trying to make

sense of his mixed messages. Her heart sank when she thought of him giving away those photos of Marty as a young man, all the still frames that had captured his life. What bothered him so much about them that he wouldn't be willing to keep them? Hannah, being a photographer, would be horrified at the mere thought of it. And Sarah knew firsthand just how much her Grandma Esther loved looking at old photographs. As she slipped further into Alzheimer's, sometimes those photos were the only things that could spark her memory.

Well, it was really none of her business. All that should matter to her was seeing that this house was in good enough order that Hannah's wedding guests wouldn't get bitten by a spider or hit in the head by a loose stone falling from the house.

"It's easy to get caught up with everyday life," she sympathized. "I try to visit my grandmother every Wednesday night, but some weeks, that's not possible."

"I've been told I work too much." He jutted his lip, considering this. "Maybe I do."

"You like what you do then?"

"I don't mind it," he said. "Ironically, I ended up doing exactly what my father wanted me to do, even though I always said I'd never be like him. I wanted to be just like Marty instead."

"Do you still?" she asked, but he shook his head firmly.

"No," he said gruffly. His jaw set.

"It's funny how things work out," she commented,

hoping to keep her tone light. But her stomach fluttered with nerves when she considered the fate of her own career. There was no guarantee that she was going to win over Chloe again—not after losing a client—but at least she could be certain that she had done everything she could. "So, I take it you need to get back to Boston soon then? For work?"

"Technically I could work from wherever I want," Chris said. "My clients are spread out. I work from a home office. Family business."

"Ah." She frowned as she peeled back the paper of her sandwich. "So you could keep the house without impacting your career. You could live here. Have your lunch out here every day. Work in Marty's library..."

He laughed out loud. "That's a very nice fantasy. The place is a teardown, or it should be."

She couldn't deny that it was a work in progress. "Still, it seems like a shame to sell it."

"The upkeep alone would be outrageous. Believe me, I know from my clients just how much it costs to heat something that big. And those lead-paned windows don't offer the same kind of insulation as newer windows, either."

"I guess it's the romantic in me. Inheriting a seaside mansion. Discovering hidden treasure. Exploring every nook. Waking up to the sound of the waves crashing in the distance." She smiled wistfully at such a thought. "You could set up a home office right above the garage in that carriage house."

Chris was shaking his head. He'd already polished off

the sandwich and picked up an apple. "Nope. You might see the romance in it, but I see the reality."

"I guess we balance each other out then," she said, and then, realizing that she'd probably gone a little too far with that comment, felt her cheeks burn. "I mean, I just—"

"Oh, I know exactly what you meant. That photographer who came by said the same thing."

Sarah frowned. There weren't many photographers in town. "Was her name Hannah?"

He nodded. "Yeah. Hannah."

"She's the one who will be getting married here," Sarah said, feeling a sense of warmth at the notion.

Chris frowned at her. "She didn't say anything. She said how much she wished she could get married here."

"That's because I haven't told her yet," Sarah explained.

He gave her a funny look. "Well, shouldn't she know?"

"She will. I just...Well, after what happened yesterday morning, it's sort of a good thing that I didn't tell her right away."

He looked down at the sand then up at her, his gaze deep, so intense she almost looked away. "I'm a man of my word."

She nodded. She wanted to believe that. Her heart told her that she could. There was something so earnest in his eyes, in the depth of his stare. But her head... "I don't trust people easily." Or maybe she was too trusting. She'd been called naïve before. But that was the old

Sarah. The new Sarah knew that she couldn't go giving her heart away to every idea of love that came along.

No good ever came from it before.

"That makes two of us," he said wryly, shoving the apple core into the bakery bag. "So we're not opposites after all." His mouth crooked into a grin and Sarah felt her heart begin to beat a little quicker.

Something told her that she and Chris had a lot in common. And that they'd get along just fine. Or that they might have done. In another time. Another place.

She grinned to herself. So much for the romantic. She was turning into a realist. Just like the man sitting beside her.

He hadn't been out here on the beach since he'd been back to the house. And he hadn't been back to the house since Jenna had died. Seeing that photo yesterday had stirred things up. The memories of the days here on this very beach, especially the last one, which had started so perfectly, the sun shining and warm, the breeze light and cool. He hadn't thought he could come out here again, sit on the sand, stare out over the water, and face the one thing he tried not to think about, ever. But being here, with Sarah...it was easier than he'd expected.

"I enjoyed this," he admitted. "I've been a little stressed since I came back to town."

"You don't like it here, do you?" She was looking at him like he was crazy, and something told him that maybe he was. After all, what wasn't there to like about Oyster Bay, this house, this rocky shoreline with the waves crashing and the gulls soaring?

"It's a nice town," he said. "And it's a nice house. But I—"

She shook her head. "I know, I know. You don't want the upkeep. You raise a good point, you do."

"It's more than that," he admitted, surprised to hear the words said aloud. He could have said nothing, bagged the rest of their lunch, and headed back up to the house. But he didn't want to go back, not yet, and not because the mere thought of all that dust was enough to make his eyes burn. He was calm out here. And Sarah...she was easy to talk to. Open. Honest. It was refreshing.

He remembered what she had said, that day in town. That's how people were here in Oyster Bay. They sure weren't that way back in Boston. Or maybe they were and he hadn't given them a chance to show it.

Sarah had just been more persistent. She'd worn him down. He was happy she had.

"The truth of the matter is, much as I loved Marty, I don't want to end up like him, you know? At least, not anymore."

She winced, and the honesty in her eyes told him that she did know, that she understood, even if she hadn't known Marty personally.

"He was alone, in this big old house. I know he looked forward to my visits. It's one of the reasons I feel so guilty, I suppose." There were other reasons, of course, but he didn't want to get into them now. Couldn't get into them, really. Ever.

"My grandmother vaguely knew him," Sarah said, giving him a funny look. "She said a lot of women in town were interested in him."

Chris considered this. Marty never seemed to have an interest in moving on with his life. He'd been alone for as long as Chris had known him. "Maybe so. I'm not even sure he knew that. Not sure it would have changed who he was." Chris shook his head, thinking of Marty alone at his big piano, a drink at his side. "He got set in his ways. Maybe he even liked being alone."

Maybe Chris eventually would too. Maybe there was hope for him yet, he thought.

"Maybe," Sarah said. She stood up and brushed the sand from her jeans. "But I'd hate to think of anyone choosing to be alone. Although, I've sort of done that myself lately."

Well, this was interesting. He perked up, happy for the shift in topic. "Bad breakup?"

She considered this for a moment. "Guess it's just easier to be alone sometimes. But the more I think about it, maybe it's not the best choice."

He considered this. She had a point. Not that he could admit it. Not even to himself. The easier path was sometimes the better one. Self-preservation and all that.

He looked up at her, blinking into the sun. Her tank top pushed against her stomach in the breeze. Her hair had been freed from its ponytail and now hung loosely at her shoulders. The sun was bright, shining down on them with all its intensity of the midafternoon, but the intensity of its glow seemed to catch the light in her eyes and the rosiness of her cheeks. He suddenly had the feeling that this had all been a very bad idea.

"Well, I guess we should get back to it," he said, hearing the reluctance in his tone, and not just because he loathed the thought of entering that house again, or picking up another cleaning rag, or unearthing another photo like the one Sarah had found, the one that was now tucked in the bottom of his suitcase at the hotel, in its album, where he didn't have to think about it.

The truth was that he was having a nice time, here, on the shore of all places. And he wasn't quite ready to get back to reality just yet.

Ten

"You know what we should do," Sarah said as she shook out the towel and folded it in half. "We should have a painting party."

"A painting party?" He didn't look very convinced.

"You know, spruce the place up a bit. Patch up some of the window frames and rough spots on the doors. The conservatory would be gorgeous in a warm butter yellow, and I can just picture that front parlor in a dusty rose."

"Rose? As in *pink*?" His expression evolved from shock to one of knowing. "You're thinking of the wedding!"

"I am not," she said primly as she gathered up the last of their sandwich wrappers. "I told you that this wedding was going to be held outside."

"And if it rains?"

"A tent, of course," she said. Still, she couldn't quite look him in the eye, and he held up a finger, grinning with satisfaction.

"A-ha!" he said. "You are thinking of that wedding. You're thinking of what you could use the house for."

She stopped walking, sighing in exasperation. "And is it such a bad idea? The house is vacant. No one lives there. You don't know how long it will take to sell. It could be put to use. Maybe the house was meant to be something other than a personal residence. If you don't enjoy it, at least give other people in Oyster Bay the chance to."

Chris shook his head. "I told you, I'm selling the place. And I'm not going to change my mind on that."

"Yes, sir," she said, nodding, but she was fairly certain that he could tell she didn't believe him. And why should she? This house held a lot of memories for Chris. It was part of his family history. It belonged with him.

But again, that wasn't her business, was it?

"Look, you want to sell it, and the best way to do that is to make it look its best. A fresh coat of paint wouldn't hurt anything. It would help."

"We don't have enough time," he said. "Besides, I'm not painting the front room pink."

"Dusty rose," she said, but even she couldn't fight off a smile. "And we can find the time if we work through the night. What about a warm apricot?"

"Warm apricot?" He looked equally horrified and confused. "What even is that?"

She thought about it for a minute. "Not quite peach. Not quite blush."

He stood, rooted in the sand, staring at her with an

amused glint in his eye. Still, he hadn't shut her down. Yet. "So, in other words, pink."

She shrugged. "Call it what you will, but I never used that word."

She turned and walked back toward the house, and then, turned around. "How about this? Whoever makes it to the house first gets their choice of color."

"But I never even agreed to paint."

Perhaps not, but he would. It would help the house sell. And until then, it would only make Hannah's wedding that much prettier because of course some of the guests would find a way to linger inside the house, and wouldn't Hannah and the bridal party want to use this space before the ceremony?

She sprinted through the sand at full speed, which wasn't saying much considering she'd been the worst kid on the track team two years in a row and had only joined to have an excuse to spend time with Justin Sloane, a junior with a steady girlfriend. In other words, a waste of her emotions. When she reached the path to the lawn, she took the steps two at a time, her thighs feeling like they might give out. She'd gotten a head start, but not by much, and Chris pushed past her at a speed she knew she couldn't top, but that didn't stop her from trying.

Wishing she'd tied on her gym shoes first instead of clutching them to her chest, she gave a gallant effort right up until the point that Chris slapped the handle of the door to the kitchen and grinned triumphantly.

She reached the terrace and stood, panting, her heart pounding from both apprehension and the exercise. She really needed to make more time for the gym. And, considering that she no longer had to go extra slowly on the treadmill lest she break a sweat while she roved her eyes around the room looking for an eligible man, she would be in better shape in no time. She might even enter next fall's Turkey Trot. Chloe entered every year. But then, Chloe was regimented that way.

"I win," Chris declared, and damn it, he wasn't even out of breath. She curled her lip. She should have known better than to suggest a race. The man was clearly in shape, and likely hit the gym a few times a week. His lean muscles were proof of it. Not that she was looking.

"Just hear me out," she said, but her words came out in gasps, and she sputtered on a cough. She composed herself, ignoring the gleam in his eye, and said, "Sorry. I'm uh, not much of a runner."

"So I've noticed," he commented. He was looking at her with curiosity. "So why offer up the challenge?"

"Because I thought I could take you," she said, because for some reason she thought she might, if she tried hard enough. That was just the problem with her, perhaps. She dared to dream, instead of accepting a situation for what it was.

"And because I think that we should paint a few of the rooms," she said. "We should put fresh flowers in as many rooms as possible too."

"Flowers!" But she could tell she had him considering it.

"You aren't just having this estate sale to earn money," she pointed out. He'd made that more than clear. "You need the place to look its best. For some people, it will be their first and only chance to see the inside of this house."

"I'm beginning to wonder if Jim is giving you a slice of his commission," Chris said. He leaned back on the doorjamb, looking out into the garden. "I don't mind if you cut some of these flowers. The roses, maybe?"

Now it was her turn to gape. "Cut the roses? Absolutely not! Those roses have to be there for Hannah's wedding! No. We will buy flowers. In town. I'm friends with the florist."

"And the paint?" he asked.

Her heart started to speed up. She licked her bottom lip, not wanting to appear too eager. "I can pick that up in town, too."

"We may as well go together," he said with a shrug. "You rode your bike again, after all."

True, that was true, but considering the work they had in front of them, it would have made sense for one of them to run the errand and the other to stay behind.

He wanted to go into town together. She would not be reading into that. After all, the man was probably procrastinating the work ahead of them. And there was no way that he'd know what color dusty rose was.

Right. There wasn't anything more to it than that.

Chris parked his car at the edge of Main Street and hopped out. The sidewalks were busy, full of mothers with young children and retired couples holding hands. Sometimes he used to look at couples like that and wonder if that would be him and Jenna someday. But those thoughts had passed with time, just like the pain had lessened. Now, thinking of it, he felt a wave of guilt.

He slid his sunglasses down. There was no other way to hide in a town this small. Everyone waved or said hello as they walked by. A few people knew Sarah by name. He was happy to be out, away from the dust and the memories of that old, run-down house, and he slowed his pace, taking in the storefronts.

"We should hurry," Sarah said, quickening her pace as they passed a shop that had topiaries in the front, the formal kind that his mother kept outside their family home in Cambridge.

"Bayside Brides," he said, reading the sign above the door. He looked at it with interest. "Is that where you work?"

She glanced toward the storefront and then fixed her eyes straight ahead. "Yep."

He stopped, lingering to take a longer look at the shop. Three wedding dresses were displayed in the window and through it he could see a frilly shop, with white chandeliers, pale blue walls, and an oversized flower arrangement that he hoped wouldn't be similar to what Sarah had in mind for Crestview.

"Nice place," he said. "I imagine you guys get a lot of business this time of year."

She nodded, still moving, not seeming to want to discuss it, and then, after a delay said, "Yes. It is quite busy. We used to only sell dresses and accessories, but we've expanded to wedding planning and custom gowns." Her eyes seemed imploring. "We really should hurry."

True, they should, but now she'd made him curious. "You didn't need to be at work today?" He hadn't considered this. "Are you on vacation this week?"

"Sort of." Her glance was skittish when she looked at him, but a smile broke out on her face when they approached the next block. "Ah. Here we are. Morning Glory. Best flowers in Oyster Bay. Well, only flowers in Oyster Bay, but—"

She reached for the brass handle, only to drop it again, and then quickly shuffled backward and hurried down the next side street.

He stared at her, trying to understand what she was doing, and then walked closer to the flower shop window. He peered in, looking for a guy about their age, an ex-boyfriend, no doubt, but all he saw were two women talking at a counter near the back of the room.

"Sarah!" He looked down the street for her. Honestly, this was ridiculous. They had a lot to do, and she was running off on him?

"Shh!" she hissed loudly, looking so panicked that he pulled away from the shop window and jogged toward where she was now hiding, as best she could, behind a maple tree.

"What's going on? Who are we hiding from?"

She swallowed hard. Her big blue eyes looked on the verge of tears. "My boss," she finally said.

And then it dawned on him. "Did you call in sick? Did you play hooky to help me out at the house?" He almost felt bad, until he remembered their deal. The one she had struck.

But Sarah was shaking her head. She chewed her thumbnail. Her eyes seemed big, worried under the hood of her lashes as she looked up at him, and he felt something in him shift. Something that he wanted to push back in its place nearly as much as he wanted to hold onto it. "It's not that. I'm...I'm in trouble at work."

He would have laughed out loud if she didn't look so forlorn over that statement. "You're in trouble at work?" He shook his head. She was having a go at him. "I don't believe it. You're a hard worker. I'd hire you."

She grinned at him, but he could still see the hesitation in her eyes. "I messed up. I did something stupid. My boss suggested I take the week off to decide if the position is still right for me. That's how I had the time off to help with the house."

"Is she the blonde or the brunette?" It was all he remembered of the women he saw through the window.

"The blonde," she said miserably. "So maybe you can just look up the street and tell me once she leaves the shop?"

"I can do that, once you tell me what you did to tick her off."

She glared at him. "So now you're striking a deal?"

He shrugged. "Why not?"

"Fine." She sighed as she leaned against the tree

trunk. "I went into work the other day and said that... well, that I didn't believe in love."

He felt his eyebrows pop up. So she wasn't looking for romance. Now, to find out why.

"And a client heard," she added, looking up at him miserably.

He let out a low whistle. "That probably didn't go over well."

"It didn't." Sarah pursed her lips, her eyes shifting to the side as if she were reliving the events of that day. "And now I have to find a way to make Chloe believe that I'm a good fit for the business. That I want to be there. That's why I pushed so hard to have that wedding at your estate. Chloe's planning the event for our friend Hannah. Her venue fell through and she always loved Crestview's garden."

"And you thought this might convince your boss to let you keep your job."

She nodded. "Are you still willing to help me?"

He frowned at her. "You're the one helping me. And between you and me, I'm happy that your boss told you to take the week off."

She gave him a rueful smile, and he was happy to see that she had relaxed a bit. "Ah, so it worked out for you that I got in trouble so I could help you fix up the house?"

"No, it worked out for me that you got in trouble so —" He stopped himself. He'd almost said what he'd been thinking. That he was grateful she got in trouble so that he could meet her. Spend time with her. But he couldn't say that any more than he could think it. Just like Sarah, he wasn't looking for love. He was just looking to sell his house and go back to Boston. "So that you could help me paint."

She rolled her eyes, but he could tell she was pleased. A moment later, he saw the blonde walk across the street and disappear out of view.

"I think the coast is clear," he said, jutting his chin toward Main Street.

"We should hurry," she said, moving past him. "We have a lot of work to do and not much time left before the sun goes down."

Not much time left in general, Chris realized, frowning to himself. Not much time left before the estate sale.

Not much time left with Sarah.

Posy looked up with obvious interest when they pushed into the shop a few minutes later. "You just missed Chloe!" she said, smiling broadly. Her eyes kept darting to Chris.

Sarah would have to explain him. But not yet.

"Oh, did I?" So she gathered that Chloe hadn't revealed the situation over at Bayside Brides, or Sarah's suspension, because that's what it was, really. She had been *suspended*.

She could close her eyes with shame. But she wouldn't. Not if she wanted to fix up that house in time for Hannah's wedding. After all, the last thing she needed was for Chloe to think that she'd handed her a lemon.

"I'm here to order some flower arrangements. Something cheerful. Elegant."

"For a wedding?" Posy asked, reaching for an order sheet.

"For an open house, actually," Sarah said, and immediately she saw the confusion in Posy's face. "This is my friend, Chris Foster. He's holding an estate sale at Crestview Manor this weekend."

Friend. It seemed a little presumptuous to use that word, but it felt true in a way, and Chris didn't seem to balk at the term. Instead, he smiled warmly and held out his hand to Posy, whose cheeks went a little pink when she took it.

"Estate sale! I'll have to check it out."

"You should," Chris said eagerly. "And tell all your friends."

Sarah didn't have the heart to tell Chris that all of Posy's friends were her friends, too, and that none of them could afford to buy that house, so instead she led him to a table of seasonal arrangements to get his opinion. "I'm thinking we should put one on the big table in the front hall. One in the dining room for sure. A few for the mantles. How many are there in total?"

He looked at her blankly. "Heck if I know."

She laughed. "I've counted three downstairs at least, although one is in your uncle's study, and I doubt we need flowers in there."

Posy approached the table with a look of interest. "Did you need this by a certain day?"

"Saturday morning, if that works for you," Sarah said. "I know it's short notice." And it was wedding season. Off the top of her head, she could think of at least a dozen brides who had weddings this month.

She pushed back the stab of envy. Her time would come.

Or it wouldn't. And somehow, she'd just have to stop feeling disappointed by that.

"Saturday will work," Posy said. Her eyes lingered for a moment on Chris and then widened slightly on Sarah. "Will you be picking them up or should I drop them off?"

"I can pick them up," Sarah said. She glanced at Chris. "On the way to your place."

Now Posy looked like she was nearly going to burst from curiosity. "Saturday it is then."

Sarah gave her a small smile. They seemed to be communicating in some sort of code. "Saturday." Meaning, Saturday all of Posy's questions would be answered unless she tried to call Sarah before then.

The phone rang and Posy reluctantly went back to her post at the counter to take the call, leaving Sarah alone with Chris once more. She could tell that she wasn't going to get very far asking for his opinion on matters, and that he probably didn't care if there were flowers or not; he was just following her suggestion.

He trusted her. Her taste or her judgment, she

couldn't be sure. But it felt good to have someone believe in her. If only Chloe could follow his lead...

"I'll put together some ideas and text them to Posy on the drive home," she said, glancing at what was available. Something fresh and large in scale would probably be best. Nothing too stuffy to underscore the overly formal nature of the house. Some freesia would be nice. Maybe some hydrangea, too. Sunflowers in the kitchen would be cheerful.

And peonies. She stopped to drink in the smell of a particularly lovely arrangement of peonies in various shades of pink. "Oh, how I love peonies."

"Never heard of them," Chris said gruffly.

She blinked at him. He had never heard of peonies? "Then I guess you've never been married—"

She stopped herself. Closed her eyes. Remembered what her grandmother had said and the photo she had found. Chris had been married before. But maybe, unlike pretty much every bride who came through their shop, peonies were not a contender for her bouquet.

"Peonies are a huge favorite with our clients at Bayside," she said quickly. She turned and glanced behind her, waving at Posy who was still on the phone, looking pained at the fact that they were leaving and she still didn't quite know what to make of the situation.

Sarah almost had to laugh. Posy would be mighty disappointed come Saturday when she learned just how unromantic the situation was. There was no situation. Not really. It was a deal. Nothing else.

But when Chris set a hand on her elbow and stopped

her in her tracks, her stomach took on a life all of its own. She stared at him, wondering if he was going to send her home then and there, no flowers, no paint swatches, nothing but another accusation that this had all been a giant mistake.

Instead, he grinned, and the corners of his eyes went all crinkly. And damn it if her heartbeat didn't do a little dance over that.

"Thanks, Sarah. I really couldn't do this without you." He squeezed her arm, and for a moment their eyes met and her stomach went all funny and fluttery.

She swallowed hard, mustering up a smile.

She could almost fall for him. But she wouldn't.

Eleven

Melanie had left three voicemail messages by the time Sarah bumped into her leaving her apartment on Friday morning. She'd barely had the energy to even shower last night before collapsing into bed, and she had to admit that she was dodging another round of suggestions from Melanie that she give love another chance.

She was dressed for another long day of hard, physical work: cut-off shorts, sneakers, and a tank top with a hoodie pulled over it for now, before the sun came out in full force. Melanie, on the other hand, was dressed for Bayside Brides. A navy sheath with a statement necklace in shades of rose gold and peach, and gold strappy heels that showed off a fresh pedicure.

Sarah stifled a sigh as she approached her friend, who was waving with enthusiasm. "Sorry I haven't returned your calls," she said wearily. "I've been sort of busy this week."

"I'll say!" Melanie's eyes raked over her. Since coming

to Oyster Bay and having a few fashion lessons from Abby Harper, Sarah rarely dressed in such casual clothes anymore. Melanie was onto her.

Sarah supposed she could blame it on a funk, being about to lose her job and all that, but there was no reason to keep secrets from Melanie. Melanie could be trusted.

"I've been working on Chris Foster," she started, but by the excitement that immediately filled Melanie's face, it was clear that her wording had been misinterpreted. "Not like that! For the wedding!"

Melanie didn't look convinced. "Go on."

"I've struck a deal with him. I help him get his house in order; he lets us have Hannah's wedding there."

Now that got Melanie's attention. Her eyes went wide. "Are you serious? Does Hannah know yet? Chloe?"

Sarah shook her head and zippered her hoodie. It was still cool outside, but within an hour or two, she knew the sun would be in full force. And that house would be stifling.

"No, and I'm not planning on telling them yet. Not until I've seen the bargain through."

"That makes sense," Melanie agreed. "Right now I think they're still resigned to the Harper House Inn. But you need to let them know soon. The wedding is two weeks from tomorrow." Melanie transferred her tote to her other shoulder. Sarah could see her sketch-book peeking out from the top—a reminder that Melanie's life had fallen into place. She had a secure job that she loved, and she'd found love with her oldest friend.

It reminded Sarah of how vastly different her circumstances were.

"The estate sale is this weekend, and I'll tell Chloe right after that," she said. She was so close, but she had to see it through first. "Will you be able to stop by?"

Melanie shook her head. "I wish. With you gone, Chloe and I both have to cover the store on Saturday and Sunday, and that means we have to fit all of our other clients in during after-hours."

Sarah had to admit that she was secretly pleased to hear this. Still, another shop girl could be found. She had to be sure to prove to Chloe that she wouldn't have luck finding one with the same drive and passion.

"All I can say is that Chloe had better keep you on if I have anything to do with it, and I do own half the business."

Sarah shook her head. "If Chloe doesn't want me there, I wouldn't be comfortable staying. I'm just hoping that securing this venue for Hannah will be enough."

"And Chris?" Melanie arched a brow.

"We're just friends," Sarah grumbled.

"Friends." A little smile formed on Melanie's lips. "That's quite a leap from him being the giant jerk you described last time we spoke. Sounds to me like you're giving him a chance."

She had, Sarah realized, whether she'd wanted to or not.

"Well, I've gotten to know him better—" Sarah started, but it was no use. Melanie looked far too satisfied for her own good right now, and if Sarah didn't know any better, she might even say her friend was gloating. "And I can assure, you, Melanie, that he is not looking for a relationship. He told me so."

Melanie didn't seem fazed. "So? You said the same and we both know that's not true."

Sarah opened her mouth to protest, but before she even bothered, she knew she'd lost that argument. And this was one time she was secretly pleased to admit defeat.

By Friday evening, they had managed to repair the peeling wallpaper in the front hall, repaint the dining room, living room, and front parlor, and touch up the cracked woodwork. The floors were polished. The curtains that remained were pulled back by tassels. The windows were tugged free and fresh air blew in off the bay. The dust was gone and Chris's eyes had finally stopped burning.

And he had Sarah to thank for all of it.

"This house hasn't looked this good since the last time I was here," Chris said as he set down his paintbrush and took in the last of the rooms. They were in the back living room, the one with a sweeping view of the gardens and the ocean. Befittingly, Sarah had recommended they paint this room a "smoky aqua," and who was he to argue any more than he could refuse the promise of a sunny, cheerful dining room if they went with a "happy, canary yellow"?

It had been a long time since he'd experienced the

simple pleasure of a woman's touch. He didn't realize until now just how much he'd missed it.

"And when was that?" Sarah tapped the lid back onto the paint can as he gathered up the tarps. "The last time you were here?"

"Years ago," he said vaguely, even though he knew the exact date. It was August twenty-first. Three years next month.

It was the day his life changed forever.

She nodded, looking like she wanted to ask more but didn't know if she should. They started speaking at the same time, and she laughed, taking the anxiety out of the awkward moment. She had a knack for that.

"You first," she said.

No. He wanted to hear what she had to say. Besides, he wasn't so sure that he wanted to keep talking about this at all. It was easier to push it away and tuck it behind him.

Never look back.

But now he'd come here, and now, looking back didn't feel nearly as scary as moving forward.

"Ladies first," he insisted.

"I was going to say that we should probably get these paint cans out to the garage with the others before I accidentally trip over one and ruin your floorboards."

"Our floorboards," he said. "You helped polish them, after all."

"Fine then." She gave him a small smile. "Still, I'm beat. And believe it or not, I am a very clumsy painter."

"You?" He couldn't believe it. If anything, she'd been

a perfectionist, making sure the shades looked right with the natural light before proceeding. Insisting on two coats when even one looked better than the yellowing white that it was covering.

"Anyway, what were you about to say?"

Oh. That. He had been about to say that it had been too long since he'd been back, that he felt bad about it and not just because he never saw Marty again. But he didn't want to say that now. He didn't want to live in regret and guilt as he had for so long.

What he wanted was to keep laughing. Keep smiling. Keep looking forward to tomorrow as he had been doing every day since Sarah started coming to the house.

"I was going to say that we should order a pizza. Extra cheese. We've earned it."

She seemed to falter slightly as she reached for another paint can, and for a moment he wondered if he had misread things, asked for too much. After all, she was just doing her part to keep up her end of the deal. Maybe that's all it had been.

And he had no right to feel so disappointed in that. But he did, and he wasn't so sure how he felt about that.

"Sorry," he blurted, shaking his head. Her day was done. She probably wanted to go home and take a hot shower. Or maybe she had a date. Most people had social lives. Calendars that were filled with places to be and people to see. He'd forgotten what that was like. Forgotten a lot of things, really. But some things he couldn't forget. Some things, he had to hold onto.

Just not this house.

"I don't mean you have to stay. We're done for the day. And—"

"And pizza sounds amazing right about now." She smiled, and a weight in his chest that he hadn't even known had been there all this time seemed to lift. He'd gotten used to it somewhere along the way, the heaviness, the hurt, and he hadn't even tried to make it go away because he'd just assumed that it wouldn't.

But it could, he now realized. If he let it.

"You know, I don't think we ate lunch," Sarah was saying as she gathered up the rest of the paint cans.

He didn't know whether to be relieved by her comment or tense. A part of him wanted to take back the offer, head back to the hotel, take a shower, order room service, and shut out the world. It was routine. It was comforting. It felt right.

And being with Sarah...it didn't feel wrong. And he wasn't quite sure how he felt about that.

He frowned at her for a minute and then, to his surprise, felt his stomach rumble. Her eyes popped and he had to laugh. "I don't think we did."

She shrugged. "I guess we just got caught up in the painting."

The painting. And other things, too. It was easy to forget about the real world when he was alone in this house with Sarah. Maybe, it was too easy. Or maybe, it was just how it was supposed to be.

∾

Because neither of them wanted to risk messing up their hard work on the house, they decided to take the pizza outside to the terrace, where they sat side by side on the stone wall, the pizza box between them.

It was still light outside, but not by much, and the porch lights only went so far. Sarah could imagine this space all lit up by lanterns and candles, with music playing and guests chatting, and flowers everywhere, filling the air with a sweet fragrance. Now she finally saw what Hannah saw in it. It wasn't a crumbling old house. It was a piece of history, and it was part of her history now, a chapter of her life spent here, all because of an arrangement she had made with a guy who was slowly turning into something more than just the temporary owner of the house.

"You know that I still haven't told Hannah that she can have her wedding here," she admitted as she picked up a floppy triangle of pizza and took a big bite. It was warm and salty and she hadn't even realized just how much of an appetite she'd worked up until she stopped chewing.

"Still don't trust me, eh?" His tone was light but his eyes were sheepish when he glanced her way.

She wasn't allowed to let him off the hook that easily. Not after he'd all but thrown her out of his house. "Well, you're starting to wear me down."

"I'm wearing you down?" He barked out a laugh. She liked the sound of it. He didn't laugh a lot, but come to think of it, he'd laughed more today.

So had she, if she was being honest with herself.

"You're the one who came to my door, more than once, to talk me into letting you have that wedding here at the estate."

"And to let me help you fix up this house," she reminded him. She took another bite. A bit of sauce dripped onto her chin and she wiped it off with the back of her hand. Chris handed her a napkin from the pile. "Thanks," she said. She glanced down at her shirt, making sure nothing had dripped onto it, even though it was probably hopeless anyway. She had four different shades of paint spackled on it. There was more, she was sure, in her hair. She was a mess.

And it was liberating not to care about that. Normally, sitting beside a guy as good-looking as Chris, she'd be nibbling at her food, sucking in her stomach, and fretting about something witty to say. She couldn't remember having a good belly laugh on a date. She couldn't remember anything but the nervous flutter.

She never liked that nervous flutter. She supposed she should be happy that her Friday night was being spent here, in a paint-stained tank top and jean cut-offs, in gym shoes instead of dainty sandals that would give her blisters all the way home.

"I'm going to miss this house," Chris suddenly said, and she glanced at him sharply, surprised by the frown that knitted his forehead. "Don't get me wrong," he corrected quickly. Too quickly. As if he were trying to cover up a slip, something he hadn't wanted to reveal, maybe even to himself. "I'm happy to sell it. Happy to put it behind me. But...I'll miss it."

She nodded thoughtfully, wondering what gave him such mixed feelings about the place. Enough time had passed that she decided to feel him out.

"Well, you make a good point about selling it. After all, it is a *lot* of work." She took another bite of pizza, and he shrugged, seeming like he wasn't quite convinced. "And it's too big for one person, like you said."

"It is," he agreed. "My Uncle Marty lived here all alone and that always saddened me." He reached for another slice, and so did she. "My father wasn't very hands-on. It just wasn't his way. But Marty...He'd toss the baseball around with me. Every day, unless it was raining. It's a small thing, but it meant a lot." He gave her a sad smile, and it sent a pang straight through her chest.

"Sometimes it's the small gestures that matter the most." She thought of her grandmother setting aside the pearls for her and smiled sadly into the darkness.

He nodded. "It's easy to take people for granted, I guess. It's easy to take time for granted. I'm more like my father than I thought I was, I think. A workaholic."

"Is that *really* why you didn't come back to the house?" she asked. She had wanted to know, earlier, when he'd first mentioned it, but then she'd started talking, interrupted him, and well...maybe it was for the best. It wasn't her business why he hadn't been back.

Or why he was so determined to leave again.

"I wish it was that simple of an excuse," he said, cracking the top on a can of beer. He held it out to her, and she shrugged.

"Why not?" She wasn't much of a beer drinker, but

then, she wasn't one to sit around in dirty clothes and inhale pizza with a cute guy either. Time for the new her.

Strangely, she was already feeling happier.

"The truth is that I was married, once, a long time ago," he finally said.

Sarah took a long sip of her beer. It wasn't bad, but she barely tasted it anyway. Her mind was somewhere else, her skin prickly and her senses alert. She felt odd, not sure if she should tell him that she already knew, but before she had to worry about responding, he said, "My wife passed away almost three years ago."

She blinked, trying to digest this information and hating herself for even stirring it up. Chris kept his eyes trained on the beer can in his hand, his expression was tight, and she didn't know what to say other than, "I'm sorry."

It was such a lame statement, but she didn't know how else to fill the silence. The pizza in her hand felt limp, and it felt callous to think about taking another bite now.

Chris helped himself to another slice now. He took a hearty bite, as if the admission had increased his appetite, relieved him of something that had been holding him back.

"We were married at Crestview," he said matter-of-factly.

"Of course," she murmured, but the whole time she couldn't help but wonder why he would be so determined to sell it, to never return, to turn his back on it. It was all he had left. Why not hold on? "But surely those are happy memories? I'm sure there are many, if you spent your summers here."

"There were," he said. His gaze took on a faraway look. "But the last day my wife and I were together was here, and we...well, it was our last normal day. A couple of months later..." He took a long sip of his beer. Silence filled the garden. In the distance, Sarah could hear the lull of the waves. Crickets were starting to chirp.

She watched him carefully, as his eyes went up to the sky and then down again, to the pizza on his paper plate, to the drink in his hand. She wanted to reach out, take the beer away, and put her hand in its place. He was telling her this for a reason, not just to make conversation or fill the evening, but because he wanted her to know. Or he wanted her to listen.

Or because maybe, just maybe, he'd been sensing something these past few days that had crept up, uninvited, unannounced. A connection.

"It's a good reminder not to take anything for granted," he finally said. "To live each day to the fullest."

Sarah frowned, wondering if that was what he did. If there was more to Chris than the workaholic he painted himself to be. More than the man who had come here alone to say goodbye to this house and all its memories, happy and sad.

"I'm probably not doing that, at least not as well as I could be." She knew what she wanted from life—a career she loved and a family of her own—but somehow she couldn't quite find a way to make that happen.

But she was trying, she told herself, looking at Chris.

Thanks to him, she was one step closer to saving her career and recommitting herself to it, too.

"Me either," he admitted in a whisper, and they both laughed, and this time, it wasn't to break the tension. This time it was because it felt right, natural, normal.

"So you haven't..." She wasn't even sure she should say it, or suggest it.

"Dated?" he finished for her. He shook his head. "No. It never felt like the right time. I have a routine now, and it works for me. My job keeps me busy."

But it wasn't what kept him away, she thought.

She nodded, the pizza settling to a weight in her stomach. "Well, you're probably eager to leave then. Just two more days."

Two more days. She didn't want to admit to herself that it saddened her, to think of him leaving, never to return, to think of walking through the gates, knowing that her time in this house—that her time with him— would be over.

Come Monday she'd be back at Bayside Brides, in a staff meeting. Maybe Chloe would let her keep her job. Life would return to normal. But somehow it didn't feel normal anymore. It felt, well, empty.

Twelve

The flower shop was empty when Sarah pushed through the door first thing Saturday morning—a bright, beautiful, sunny day with the promise of a breeze that, with any luck, could linger well into the afternoon. Posy wasted no time coming around the counter to greet her, her eyes wide, a smile creeping up the corners of her mouth.

"Everything is ready for you. Do you want me to help you load up your car?"

Sarah had already considered this scenario when she'd left her apartment. She'd purposefully parked in the alley behind the shop where her car wouldn't be visible to anyone on Main Street, or Chloe, who could be passing by on her way to work. She wasn't quite ready to tell Chloe the news about Hannah's wedding venue. She didn't know why, but something told her that instead of jumping right into this, as she had done so many times before, she should bide her time and take things slow. The estate sale hadn't even started yet. The deal wasn't completely upheld on her end. This time, she wasn't taking any chances.

"My car is around back," she said. She watched Posy carefully. She could tell her friend was itching to ask about Chris, why Sarah was helping him, and how she even knew him. And what could Sarah say? That she'd struck a bargain? That he was just a friend? That she sort of thought he might like her even if the facts said otherwise?

She was reading into things again, rather than accepting them for what they were. And that kind of thinking always got her into trouble. This time, it wouldn't. Chris had opened up to her. He'd told her his story, and she'd listened. She understood why he felt the need to say goodbye to Crestview, even if she didn't agree with it.

Even if she would miss him, more than she should.

"Perfect. We can take a look at everything and then get you on the road!" Posy seemed to stare at her, waiting for something more, but when it was clear that all Sarah was going to do today was stand with a serene smile, Posy's shoulders slumped. "Come on back," she said, leading Sarah behind the counter. "I have all the arrangements in my workroom."

Sarah followed Posy into the back half of the space, where sunlight filled a huge room filled with colorful flowers, some already tucked into vases, many lying on the large, butcher-block counter in the center of the room.

"You're so lucky to get to work in this beautiful room

every day!" Sarah took in the walls of ribbons, the shelves of vases in different shapes and sizes, and the flowers. Oh, they were all as pretty as the ones out front on display. She'd been in here many times over the past few months especially—when Posy was too busy to drop off the arrangements they ordered for the store, Sarah was all too happy to offer to run the errand, and she occasionally picked up a little something for her grandmother too—but she'd never seen the back room.

"I'm certainly busy," Posy replied. "But you have a pretty good setup, too. Working at Bayside Brides? Surrounded by all those gorgeous, frothy dresses? I'd have to be restrained from trying half of them on."

"I wish." Sarah had been tempted, quite tempted, especially by the ball gowns with the full, poufy skirts, but Chloe would never allow such a thing. Too much risk. "Besides, I get my share of wearing nice dresses, it seems. It's wedding after wedding these days!"

"Do you have a date for Hannah's wedding?" Posy looked at her with interest, no doubt thinking of Chris.

"Nope," Sarah said, and for once, she was able to admit this without a heavy heart. Maybe spending time with Chris had restored her hope—even if he wasn't the right guy for her, he was a nice guy, a handsome guy, and he seemed to like her, just as she was. Maybe someday she'd meet another guy like him. Only she wasn't so sure that he could be so easily replaced.

"Me either." Posy looked disappointed. Up until last year, she'd been in a relationship, and she was struggling to move on. "I wasn't sure if you would be bringing that guy you were with yesterday. The one from the Foster estate?"

"I'm just helping him out with the estate sale," Sarah clarified. She hadn't even dared to let herself think of inviting Chris to the wedding. He would be long gone by then. Besides, she wouldn't push her luck, not even as a friend. It had been difficult enough to get him to agree to hold the wedding at the house in the first place. And now, knowing his situation...well, she understood why he wasn't thrilled by the idea.

"How do you guys know each other?" Posy asked as she began transferring flower arrangements into boxes that would keep them steady on the short drive to Crestview. They were lovely: blue hydrangeas for the front hall, roses for the upstairs bedrooms, and a colorful variety of snapdragons that would be perfect in the parlor.

Sarah decided that this wasn't going to end anytime soon. Posy was curious, just like she would be if the situation were reversed.

But there was no good explanation. Other than the truth.

"I got to talking with him when he was handing out flyers for the estate sale," she said, hoping that this would satisfy her friend. But Posy's eyes just widened a notch and she blinked, waiting for the next part of the story. "I had a few days off work this week so I offered to help him out."

"Sort of like a side job?" Posy's brow knitted.

Sarah gave a little shrug. "Sort of. Yeah." After all, she

wasn't being paid, per se. It was more of a trade. And the benefit was far better than a paycheck. "He's a nice guy. But, he's only in town through this weekend."

Posy pursed her lips as if that was all she needed to hear. And really, it should have been all Sarah needed to hear, too.

With a sigh, she picked up one of the arrangements and carried it out to her car. It took them three trips to get everything loaded up and secure, the boxes tucked tightly together and packed with newspaper to make sure the vases didn't shift or tip in transit.

Sarah checked her watch, realizing with a start that the estate sale was in less than an hour. "I should probably go," she said.

"Have fun," Posy said, a little cheekily.

Sarah just shook her head as she pulled her sunglasses onto her face and opened the door.

Fun. It was hard work. A deal. A bargain they had struck. But somewhere along the way it had become fun, hadn't it?

The estate sale was scheduled to start at ten, and by eleven, Chris was starting to look anxious. "I guess I can just hire someone to clear out the place if no one comes by," he finally said. He'd been pacing the front hall for the better part of the hour.

"True," she said, but she sensed the hesitation in his voice. She'd sensed his hesitation all morning, ever since she'd arrived with the flowers. "The house looks beautiful. People will come. And when they do, I'm sure there's a lot here they'd like."

"Have you seen anything you wanted?" he asked, turning from the door.

She had been so caught up in the cleaning and painting, and well, conversation the last few days that she'd forgotten she had meant to keep an eye out for something for Hannah's wedding gift. Hannah would love something from this old house, she was sure of it, but not just anything. Something that fit her personality. A photograph. An old camera.

Or maybe just her own photos taken here, at her own wedding, Sarah thought with a smile. After all, what could top that?

"Did you set aside everything you wanted to keep?" Sarah asked Chris now. Even though he seemed adamant that he didn't need or want anything from this house, he'd been quiet all morning, and his smile seemed a little forced and didn't quite meet his eyes, even when she set out all the flower arrangements and they took a step back to admire them.

"There was one thing I always loved. My uncle had a watch. He wore it every day. It was old and you had to wind it up and he would let me do it when I visited as a kid. I always liked that watch."

"Did you check the bedroom?"

"I checked the usual places," Chris said, looking resigned.

"Well, then let's check the unusual places," Sarah

said, reaching for the banister. "Remember what I said about inheriting a seaside mansion? You have to explore all the nooks."

"You're not one to give up, are you?" Chris remarked, but there was a gleam to his eyes again that she hadn't seen since last night when she'd left.

The master bedroom of the house was one they had invested a lot of time in, removing the old drapes, washing the linens, setting a bouquet of roses on the mantle and another, smaller clipping from the garden on the long chest of drawers. Sarah started there, but of course, most of the drawers were empty.

"I went through those on my first day," Chris explained. "There didn't seem to be any reason to hold onto clothes, and Jim wanted the closets cleared out."

Of course. It made sense.

"Let's check another bedroom then," she said, but each of the other rooms proved the same. Bare surfaces that had been dusted and polished, and empty drawers. "What about a safe?" she asked. In a house this big, it couldn't be uncommon.

Chris frowned and led her downstairs to Marty's office, where sure enough, they found a safe behind one of the seascapes that were similar to the ones she'd found in the attic.

"Well, what do you know?" Chris shook his head in wonder.

"Do you have the combination?" Sarah asked.

"The lawyer never said anything about it. I suppose I

could call and ask. Or a locksmith." He reached for his phone, but Sarah stopped him.

"My guess is that it's a date. Something important to him." She wondered if she should even say it, and then thought, why not? She worked at Bayside Brides. It was her dream job. She loved weddings. And even her own disappointments couldn't stop her from thinking that. "A wedding anniversary perhaps?"

Chris frowned. "I don't know when he was married. It was before I was born."

Sarah walked over to Marty's desk. Next to the leather ink blotter was a single silver-plated frame. It was his wedding photo, she had seen it many times when she was cleaning this room, but now she saw the etching in the bottom. She tapped it. "There. That's the date."

Chris shrugged. "Worth a try."

He walked over to the lock and turned it a few times, laughing out loud when it clicked and then opened. "How did you know?"

Sarah shrugged. "Lucky guess."

Chris reached inside and pulled out the watch. It was gold and heavy, a big watch, a man's watch, and Sarah could see why he would love it. "That's certainly a keep-sake," she said as he turned it over in his hands.

"It has an engraving," Chris said, peering closer. "It's from Marty's wife. I never knew her."

"It's probably why he wore it every day," she said and felt her heart begin to do that little patter it always did when she watched one of those sappy movies on television.

Chris frowned, catching her, but a quirk soon lifted the corners of his mouth. "I thought you didn't believe in love and happy endings and all that," he told her.

Ah. So he'd been listening. "Well...just not in my personal experience."

"Mine either," he said a little sadly. He hooked the watch onto his wrist and admired it.

"It looks nice," she said. "Is there anything else in there?"

He reached inside and pulled out a few necklaces, some earrings, and a bracelet. "These aren't real," he said, and Sarah nodded. They were costume jewels, like the ones that they sold at the shop. "Why keep them in here?"

"Sentimental value," Sarah said. She smiled as she reached for them. They were lovely, delicate, and polished with sparkling pink gemstones. "He held onto the past."

"More like he never moved on from it." Chris gave her a strange look when she met his eyes, and for a moment, the air seemed to stall in her lungs. Just as quickly, he cleared his throat. "You can have them if you'd like. Consider it a thank you for everything."

"The only way you need to thank me is by letting me use the space for Hannah's wedding," she said, holding the jewelry out to him.

He held up a hand. "Not for cleaning the house. For...well, for helping me get through it. I thought this week was going to be pretty bad, but it was nice."

Sarah felt her cheeks flush and she turned quickly,

before he could see. "I'll go put these in my bag, for safe-keeping." She walked through to the parlor, where sunlight streamed in through the tall windows, and she almost leaped backward when she saw Dottie Joyce pressing her face against the glass.

"I think our first visitor has arrived!" she called out to Chris, who quickly met her in the hallway. She glanced up at him. "Be warned," was all she said.

Chris frowned at her but opened the door to reveal Dottie on the step, her eyes wide, her mouth pinched. Her wheels were no doubt turning.

"Sarah Preston?" she said with overt interest. "I thought I saw you through the window. My, my, what brings you here?" She looked Chris up and down, clearly approving of what she saw.

"Hello, Dottie," Sarah said, fighting off a sigh. She'd learned early into her days in Oyster Bay that in a town this small, sometimes it was best to dodge questions you didn't want to answer. Besides, how could she even continue to answer these questions? ¡There was nothing between her and Chris. And yet, there was certainly something.

"Chris Foster." Chris extended his hand. "Marty's nephew."

"My," Dottie said, blushing. "I'm Dottie Joyce, head of the Historical Society. I must say, this house appears to be in better condition than I expected. You've worked hard."

"Oh, I had a helper." Chris glanced at Sarah, giving her a grin, and Dottie's eyes positively popped.

"My!" she said again, her mouth forming a perfect little circle.

Sarah could only shake her head. "It's a beautiful house, Dottie, and I saw some seascapes that I thought you might enjoy. Some have birds, gulls, flying over the water." It was no secret after Margo had been commissioned to redecorate Dottie's home that the woman had a collection of birds: bird wallpaper, which Margo had succeeded in stripping, birdcages, and figurines of birds. "Some things might be nice to feature at the Historical Society, too."

Dottie picked up a set of candlesticks and set them down with a long sigh. "It's a shame that Oyster Bay doesn't have a museum. So much history here! So much that could have been displayed!"

"Yes, well, why don't I show you around?" Sarah offered, but it seemed that Dottie had a better idea.

"Perhaps this young gentleman might do the honor?"

Chris cut her a glance, but Sarah could only smile serenely. After all, he had been warned.

While they walked around, a few others from town stopped by, and several couples that Sarah didn't recognize as well. Tourists, no doubt. By midafternoon they had sold off most of the seascapes, Marty's old globe that sat in a corner of his office, a pile of music sheets, several mirrors, and a handful of hand-painted vases.

By the end of the day, Sarah was feeling downright optimistic, until she glanced out the window and saw a car pull up.

"Oh no," Sarah said, her heart thudding. "It's Chloe."

Chris's eyes sparked with interest as he pressed his face against the window. "Who's Chloe?"

"My boss!" She grabbed his arm to pull him back. The last thing she needed was to raise any more suspicion with Chloe. Chris's arm was warm and smooth, and she felt a rush of heat at the physical contact.

If he noticed, he didn't react, but then, he was too busy having fun with her if the amusement in his grin said anything,

"Oh, this should be good."

"No!" she warned, giving him a long, hard look that she was sure bordered more on fearful than fierce. "I'm in enough trouble already."

He leaned in closer to the glass, and this time, no amount of tugging at his arm was going to pull him away from the window. Not that she minded the effort.

"Oh, yes. The blonde that I saw coming out of the flower shop. She's looking up at the house."

Oh, God. Oh, God. What was Sarah supposed to say? She had blown her cover now. She should have excused herself, quietly, let Chris deal with Chloe, and return when the coast was clear. None would have been the wiser. But now Chris was determined to mess with her.

"She doesn't look mean," he said, turning to give her a crazy look.

Sarah shifted the weight on her feet impatiently. "I

never said she was mean. I just said she's...well, she's a perfectionist."

He raised an eyebrow. "And you're not?" He glanced back through the window and then said excitedly, "She's almost here!"

That was it. Sarah turned, hoping to make a spring for it, but now it was Chris's hand on her arm, pulling her back, and oh...it was hard to resist. Firm but soft enough to spread warmth through her body.

She went along with him, hoping he would drop his hand, and then feeling disappointed when he did. She didn't need the temptation. Besides, the last thing she needed was for Chloe to walk in to find them having some kind of wrestling match.

"Fine," she said, however reluctantly. She smoothed her shirt, pulling in a breath for courage. But when the door opened and Chloe looked around the hall, and her eyes finally locked with Sarah's, all her confidence seemed to pool at her feet.

"Sarah?" Chloe looked at her in confusion and then, more uneasily said, "Funny running into you here."

"I'm Chris Foster," Chris said, stepping forward to extend a hand. Sarah saw the flush in Chloe's cheeks as she shook it, and Sarah couldn't help but feel a wave of jealousy. Chloe was pretty. Painfully put together. Today she was wearing a simple pink shift dress that matched her perfect mani and pedi. Her metallic strappy sandals looked like they had never been worn, even though Sarah had seen her in them dozens of times. Her hair was smooth and glossy and she'd probably never experienced a split end since trims were on her calendar, booked in advance, like a dentist appointment. It wasn't that she was vain. She was just...perfect.

And Sarah, in her jean cut-offs and grey tee shirt, was far from it. And Chloe had managed to point that out, more than once now.

"Chloe Larson," Chloe said, dropping her hand.

"Chloe and I work together," Sarah said and then reddened. They did work together. Tomorrow's meeting would determine if they still did.

"Ah, so you work for the bridal salon then?" Chris said enthusiastically, and Sarah watched him warily, wondering where he was going with this, hoping that he was just being friendly, scoping out the situation before sending Chloe off to peruse what remained of the estate sale.

Sarah racked her brain to think of something Chloe might find interesting. "I saw a lovely jewelry case in one of the bedrooms that made me think of you," she said, but before Chloe could reply, Chris leaned against the doorjamb, settling in for a nice long chat.

Oh, no.

"Well, I hope the weather cooperates for the wedding you're planning," Chris said casually.

Sarah's eyes burst open. No! He wasn't supposed to say anything. Not yet. Not when Sarah hadn't even told Chloe yet. She was saving it, for Monday's meeting. Except now, she wasn't sure why she was putting it off. Chris had proven he was keeping up his end of the bargain, and she had certainly kept up hers, if three split nails, an aching back, and overwhelming fatigue said anything.

"Wedding?" Chloe glanced at Sarah in confusion. "What wedding?"

Here it went. Sarah licked her bottom lip and took a deep breath. "Mr. Foster has agreed to let us use the space for Hannah's wedding."

Oh, the look on Chloe's face. What Sarah would have done at that moment to have had her cell phone handy so she could snap a photo, but the memory of it would be seared in her memory, she was sure. Half surprise, half astonishment. Total disbelief.

"I didn't agree at first," Chris said, grinning over at Sarah. "But Sarah convinced me. She must be quite an asset to your business."

Chloe said nothing, but just nodded, blinking in confusion as she stood in the hallway, trying to process everything. Finally, she said, "Have you told Hannah yet?"

Sarah would have loved nothing more than to tell the Donovan sisters the news, but she knew that technically, it wasn't her place. "You're planning the event for Hannah. I figured you should be the one to tell her."

Something unreadable passed through Chloe's eyes, and she made her excuses before slipping into the front parlor. Sarah sunk against the wall in relief, but she couldn't deny the flutter when she caught Chris looking at her across the room.

"Thank you," she whispered, her heart bursting with relief and gratitude.

He gave a modest shrug as he stuffed his hands into his pockets, but she could tell he was pleased. "So I guess I'll see you in the morning?"

"Bright and early," she said, looking forward to it almost as much as she hated to leave.

And almost as much as she hated to believe that Melanie was right: she had given a guy who wasn't her regular type a chance, and she'd gone and fallen for him.

Chris winked at her and then walked into the dining room, leaving her alone in the bright, sunny entryway of a house that had suddenly started to feel an awful lot like home. If only Chris could see it that way too.

Thirteen

News of the estate sale must have spread because, by Sunday morning, there were four cars in the driveway ten minutes before the designated start time. Dottie came back for the rest of the seascapes, as Sarah suspected she would, and the Harper and Donovan sisters stopped by to celebrate the good news that Chloe had shared.

"I still can't believe it," Hannah kept saying, over and over again. "When the winery flooded, I thought my wedding was ruined, but now...Well, it's like it was meant to be."

Sarah had smiled to herself, wondering if such a thing were true. Once she would have said so, and a week ago she wouldn't have, but this week, well she almost dared to believe in fate again.

Margo picked out some items for a client whose dining room she was designing—a curio cabinet with clean lines that she said she would paint white—and Bridget bought a few crystal bowls for the inn.

"Do you have anything here related to photography?" Hannah asked, and Sarah was about to say that she hadn't seen anything, when Chris nodded.

"There's a trunk of old photos in the attic," he said, catching her eye briefly before looking away.

Sarah waited until her friends had gone up the stairs in search of these tempting items before pulling Chris aside. "I thought you got rid of those."

"I kept the ones that I should," he said, and she left it at that. She'd opened a wound the other day, but maybe, just maybe, it was starting to heal, at least a little.

"Well, I'd like to see these photos! Some of them might be old, and show some history of the town," piped in Dottie Joyce, who seemed to have a knack for eavesdropping on every conversation.

"Certainly," Chris said. "Take the stairs to the top. And mind the mice," he added in a whisper so low that only Sarah could hear.

"You're terrible," Sarah said, laughing. "Besides, that mouse was in the bedroom, not the attic."

He cocked an eyebrow. "Where do you think it came from?"

She felt the blood drain from her face until she realized he was joking. She swatted his arm, giving him a rueful look, but just when her heart started to flutter it turned over just as quickly.

Today was it. The last day. And tomorrow...No thinking about that, she told herself firmly, as she went upstairs to the attic to make sure that Chris was indeed only joking, and that Dottie Joyce wouldn't be scared out of her wits by the sight of a rodent who may or may not bite.

By the time the estate sale was over, Sarah calculated that close to half the town had come through. "Likely for a look-see," Chris said, giving her a look.

It was true that not everyone had left with something, and some, like Jim McDowell and his wife Trish, came in support.

"This house has been a part of Oyster Bay for generations," Sarah said. "Can you blame people for wanting to get a peek behind the iron gate?"

"I guess that Marty did cut himself off," Chris admitted.

"Besides, we did pretty well," Sarah said, walking through the rooms. They were still furnished, but most of the clutter had been cleared, between the trash pickup and the sale. Most people left with a smile on their faces. "There may have been a prospective buyer in the group, too."

For some reason, Chris didn't look as thrilled by this prospect as she'd expected. Was he still disappointed that a few oversized oil paintings hung on the walls?

"Jim seemed pleased with the house," she pointed out, thinking of his remarks about the quick improvement.

"He did love the wall colors," Chris admitted. "I

think that calls for a celebration. Dinner on me? You pick the place."

It's not a date, it's not a date, she told herself over and over again, but this time, she couldn't push that thought away. This time, it was different. This time, if she didn't know better, it was a date.

"Let's go someplace where we can sit outside. We've been cooped up a lot these past few days. Not that I minded," she added, lest she inadvertently imply that the past few days had been some sort of hardship. They'd been surprisingly pleasant, eye-opening, and wonderful really. And now, they had come to an end.

"I haven't minded either," he said, holding her gaze.

She dropped hers to the floor, feeling a flush heat her cheeks. "Right. So. Dinner. French, Italian, or seafood? I don't know if you've heard about the Main Street expansion. They've opened some new places recently."

"You pick," he said as they stepped outside into the late afternoon sunshine.

"Okay, then, seafood," she said. "Hannah's dad owns The Lantern. It's one of my favorite places in town." She was craving a good lobster salad and she no longer felt the need to feed into a cliché of a first date at a cozy French bistro with a candle flickering on the table. Love wasn't all about flowers and chocolates, she'd realized these past few days. It was about companionship. Partnership. Maybe even a little perseverance.

What was she saying? She didn't love Chris. And this wasn't a first date.

But she could love him, she knew, and that...well,

that was bittersweet, wasn't it? He'd opened her heart again. And that might just have to be enough.

She turned, trying to fight the weight in her chest when she looked back up at the big house. "Is it okay to say that I'm going to miss this place?"

"You'll be back again in two weeks, though," he cajoled. "For your friend's wedding."

"True," she said, but it did little to lift her spirits. "But it won't be the same."

He looked over at her, really looked at her, and she could tell that he was searching for more, for a hint into what she had meant. But there wasn't an answer, not a simple one at least. She would miss this past week. The hard work. The simple thrill of a goal being achieved. The teamwork.

But most of all, she'd miss him.

"I'd like to think that this isn't goodbye," he said, his voice low and gravelly, and even though the old Sarah would have analyzed that comment a hundred ten ways four times over again, she knew there was no mistaking what he meant.

He'd miss the house, too. What it was. What it had become. What they'd shared.

And maybe, just maybe, like her, he wasn't quite ready for it all to be over quite yet.

Sarah rode her bike home with enough time to change into something for dinner. She swapped out her shorts and tee shirt for a sundress. Her hand lingered on the hanger of the dress she'd bought for the online date that had never happened, and she pondered just how much had happened in such a short period of time—and how much could change so quickly.

She set the dress aside, deciding she would give it to Abby as a gesture to return all the clothes and accessories that Abby had lent or given to her over time. She wanted tonight to be a fresh start. A new chapter.

An hour later, she was back on Main Street, this time by foot, a lightness in her step when she considered that in just a few minutes she'd be seeing Chris again. The Lantern was at the end of the street, and she didn't even flinch when she passed Bayside Brides which was closed by now, of course. Still, she thought she saw a light on in the back room. No doubt Chloe was still working hard. This time tomorrow, Sarah would be back inside those four walls, the classical music playing softly over the speakers, surrounded by beautiful gowns.

She'd missed the place, but she'd miss Chris more, she thought sadly.

She was just coming up to Books by the Bay when Trish was closing up shop. "Hey, Trish," she said, stopping for a moment to chat. She was running early, and there was no sense in sitting at a table by herself for ten minutes. The old Sarah was eager like that. It hadn't gotten her anywhere.

"That was quite an estate sale!" Trish said, dropping the keys into her handbag. "I managed to get some gorgeous brass bookends. They'll look great in my next window display."

"I found something too, actually," Sarah said. "Some beautiful antique jewelry."

"Chloe will be impressed!" Trish said, giving her a knowing look. They both knew how difficult it was to impress Chloe.

Sarah said, "Actually, it's for me. It was a thank you from Chris. For helping him out."

"And that you certainly did!"

"I'm on my way to meet Chris for some drinks right now," Sarah said and rolled her eyes when Trish gave her a knowing look. "It's not like that. He's going back to Boston tomorrow," she said firmly, not just to Trish, but to herself.

"So Chris was pleased with the turnout then?" Trish joined her as they began walking down Main Street toward The Lantern.

Sarah nodded. "Hopefully it helps Jim show the place," she said. She could only imagine what the commission on that would mean for their family.

"Well, you're not the only one celebrating tonight. I'm probably the first to know, but Jim just presented Chris with an offer."

Sarah's pulse skipped. "A buyer? So soon?"

Trish was beaming as she nodded her head. "I know! Jim was just as surprised as the rest of us. But someone came through the sale and saw real potential in the place. I doubt they would have a week ago."

No, probably not, Sarah thought.

"Wow." Sarah's mind was spinning, and it was only then that she realized that up until now she'd been holding out hope, just like she'd promised herself not to do anymore. She'd romanticized it in her mind, a fantasy of Chris keeping the house, staying in town. Having a change of heart.

Opening his heart.

She almost didn't dare herself to ask the question she wanted to ask, the one that would cement herself in denial. Did he accept the offer?

The question played over and over again in her mind until she forced it away, along with the hope. Of course he had said yes! He'd come to town to sell the house. He had never implied otherwise.

Instead, she asked, "When does the sale close?"

"They want possession as soon as possible, apparently," Trish said. "It's a cash offer, so if everything proceeds smoothly, it should all be finalized by next week."

"Next week?" But Hannah's wedding was a week from Saturday. Chris would never have agreed to that, surely! He was a man of his word; he'd said that over and over, and she'd finally believed him.

But he'd said other things, too. Things that didn't fit with what her heart wanted to hear.

Her heart was pounding so loudly that she was sure that Trish could hear it, but Trish seemed completely pleased, and perhaps she expected Sarah to be too. But how could she? Now Hannah wouldn't get her wedding venue. Now Sarah might not be able to keep her job.

She'd believed in him. She'd opened her heart.

And he'd broken it.

"I'm sorry, Trish, I have to run." Her voice was shaky and she could barely even look her friend in the eye. She didn't know where she had to go or what she could even do, but she had to get away, to think. "It was good talking." It wasn't good. It was only good to know. And even then, she wasn't sure she wished that she had ever known.

She hurried away, down the sidewalk, past Bayside Brides, looking to cross the street before she approached the Oyster Bay Hotel, but it was too late. There was Chris, coming out the front door, his hands in his pocket, a smile on his face.

Anger swelled within her.

"Sarah!" He was grinning, ear to ear, his eyes shining with more happiness than she'd seen all week. "I was just coming to meet you."

"Coming to gloat?" Her heart panged when his expression dropped, but she pushed away the guilt and doubt she felt when she saw the confusion in his eyes. "I heard all about the offer from Jim's wife. We're friends. Everyone in town is friends. That's what makes it such a great place to live."

Chris sighed heavily and looked down at the pavement. "I was going to tell you."

"Oh, I'm sure you were. Because you're a man of your word." She was blinking back tears, but she would be damned if she cried over another man who didn't deserve her. "And I was stupid enough to believe you. Believe in you. I thought... I thought we had something."

He looked at her sharply. "We do have something, Sarah. If circumstances were different. In another time, another place."

She stared at him, trying to understand what he was

saying, and the pain in his expression told her everything she needed to know. He did like her. But he just wasn't willing to start anything between them.

"There is no other time or place," she said. "There's just today."

He shook his head, and her heart felt like it broke just a little bit more. "But it doesn't change the facts."

"And what are the facts?" she asked, crossing her arms over her chest. Her eyes burned into his and she waited to see if he would waver, maybe even held out hope to see what he would say.

"That house has bad memories for me."

"And good ones, too," she pointed out.

He lowered his eyes as if he still couldn't admit that, or focus on it. "I can't keep holding onto the past," he finally said.

"But that's exactly what you're doing," she told him, her voice starting to shake with emotion. "Selling that house won't help you move on with your life. That house is just a thing, a place. It doesn't change how you live or how you feel."

He glanced up at her, saying nothing. "I don't want to end up like Marty, alone in that house, mourning the past."

She shook her head. "But you're just like Marty," she said softly. She didn't know why she hadn't seen it before. It was so obvious, all along, and she'd reverted to her old ways, dared to be a dreamer instead of a realist. "You're alone, fixated on the past, unwilling to move forward or let people in. That house has nothing to do with it."

"Maybe you're right," he surprised her by saying.

"So, you're going to turn your back on your uncle and all your memories, just like you turned your back on me and our deal?"

"It's not that simple," he said, his jaw setting.

"Actually, Chris, it is that simple. Sometimes in life, you have to make a choice. You can sit at home, all by yourself, locked in the past, afraid to live, or you can open your mind, and give something new a chance."

But it didn't always work out, she thought to herself. There was no guarantee.

She'd taken a chance. Not just on working out her professional life. She'd taken a chance on her heart, even though she hadn't planned on it.

"I have to go, Chris," she said, turning away, and this time, she didn't look back.

Fourteen

It was a typical Monday morning in Oyster Bay. The sun was shining. The gulls were swooping down over the Atlantic. Tourists had flocked back to their hometowns, leaving the streets quiet and sleepy. Shop owners on Main Street tended to the flowers that flanked their front doors, taking their time in turning their signs, the start of a new week brewing just as quickly as the coffee she could smell from the paper cup from Angie's that she clutched in her hand.

But there was nothing typical about this Monday to Sarah, she thought as she stood outside of Bayside Brides and took a deep breath. There was no avoiding it. Today was the day she was meant to check-in, and it was the day she would learn her fate.

The shop wasn't open yet, of course. There was the Monday meeting to get through, if she made it that far. She'd considered calling Melanie last night, crying over a drink with her, telling her everything that had transpired, how close she had been, but it didn't seem fair to ruin Melanie's weekend that way. That was something the old Sarah would do.

This was her mess to clean up. She would deal with Chloe, alone. She would walk out of here today, either in an hour, or seven hours, but she would still walk. She'd done her best. She had no regrets.

Well, almost none.

Chloe was arranging the jewelry in the case when Sarah entered the store. The jewelry. Sarah had nearly left what she'd taken from the estate sale at home, but the sight of it was a painful reminder of how quickly things could turn, and not always for the better. No, it was better here, in the display case, rather than stuffed inside her top drawer. Someone would come along and buy it. It would bring them happiness. They'd make new memories from it.

"Good morning!" Her tone was nearly cheerful but not quite. She looked around for Melanie. No sign of her yet.

"Sarah!" Chloe's tone held just a note of surprise, but she was pleasant when she smiled. "How did the rest of the sale go?"

Anxiety came in waves as she managed a tight smile. Had Chloe remembered their arrangement? Was she expecting her today? Or did she assume Sarah had too much pride to fight for what she wanted?

Fight for what she wanted. That's what she'd done all week. Before that even. She wasn't a quitter.

"I brought something from the Crestview estate

sale," she said, reaching into her tote for the small cloth bag she'd set the items in this morning. "They're vintage. Costume jewelry, of course. But some are unique." She set the earrings, bracelet, and two necklaces on the glass cover, her heart panging as she released the last earring from her hand.

"These are stunning!" Chloe leaned in to admire them. "Are you sure you don't want to keep them for yourself?"

Sarah wondered if the strain showed in her eyes as she forced a smile. "Oh, I don't have a reason to hold on to them. These would be perfect for one of our brides."

"They would," Chloe agreed. She gave her a smile that almost passed for apologetic, but felt sincere. "Thank you."

Sarah nodded and swallowed hard. That had been the easy part. The hard part—the part where she told Chloe that she hadn't secured the Foster estate for Hannah's wedding after all—was still looming.

Chloe locked up the case and slid the estate jewelry into her palm. "I'll clean these and tag them, too. I might have a chat with Bob down at the antique shop to see if they're worth anything first, although I imagine that they would have snagged them first if they were."

"Chris gave these to me before the estate sale started," Sarah said, hoping to gloss over the details of that exchange. "They were in the safe, so you never know. But, I think they're costume jewelry."

Chloe eyed her with interest. "You and Chris seem to have become close."

"Nothing is going on between the two of us," Sarah told her.

Chloe didn't look convinced, but she turned and walked toward the back room, and Sarah, staving off a fresh bout of nervous energy, set a hand to her stomach and closed her eyes. This was it. The moment when she revealed her latest disappointment. The moment when she might be fired, once and for all.

"Is Melanie here this morning?" she all but squeaked, even though it was obvious. No Melanie.

"She had an urgent call from her difficult client this morning," Chloe said, pausing to roll her eyes as she reached for the door of the back room.

Of course. And knowing just how difficult and time-consuming Samantha King could be, it was fair to conclude that Melanie wouldn't be here in time for the meeting today—not any part of it.

She followed Chloe into the now beautifully renovated storage room and took her usual seat at the table, dread building as she waited for Chloe to do the same. But of all times, Chloe turned to her and said, "Tea?" and Sarah fought back the urge to prolong this conversation as much as she wished to get it over with once and for all.

"Sure," she managed.

She regretted her decision immediately, as she sat in agony, watching as Chloe filled the electric kettle, flicked it on, and pulled two mugs from a small cabinet. She made small talk, about clients, about the latest shipment of sample dresses, and Sarah heard herself murmuring and commenting even though her mind was spinning and she was now truly panicking and the last thing she cared about was what color Samantha had finally chosen for her bridesmaids.

"I'm glad we're meeting," Chloe said as she finally set the two steaming mugs of tea on the table (but not before first getting two coasters from a drawer) and took the chair across from Sarah.

"Me too," Sarah said, leaning forward. She opened her mouth. "There's something—"

But Chloe held up a hand. "I should apologize."

Oh no. No, not this. Sarah felt like she could start to cry. This wasn't how it was supposed to go. She was supposed to come in here, blurt out the fact that they would have to find a new venue for Hannah, and then Chloe would either fire her then and there or agree to keep her on, and over time, the tension would subside.

A heart-to-heart was never in the cards. And yet, here it was...

"I feel bad about how I reacted," Chloe said. "You didn't behave professionally, but neither did I. We're a team at Bayside Brides, and you've certainly shown your passion for the business over time. I shouldn't have questioned that."

Sarah said nothing. What could she say? Everything that Chloe was saying was true. She'd just never expected to hear it.

"I accused you of bringing your personal issues into the store, but the truth is that I'm guilty of this myself." Chloe gave her a sheepish look.

Sarah frowned. "I don't understand." Chloe was nothing if not professional.

Chloe pressed her palms to the table. As always, her nails were manicured. This week's color was a soft ballet pink. "I sometimes take this business too seriously. I sometimes...overreact."

Now Sarah sat frozen at the table. It wasn't like Chloe to show emotion. Sarah hadn't even been sure she possessed it. But now she saw a crack in the careful shell that Chloe lived in.

"I let my issues and emotions interfere with how I'm running this business. Melanie pointed this out to me, and she's right. I'm not perfect. No one is. I want this to be an enjoyable place to work. For all of us. At the end of the day, I think we're all here for the same reason."

Sarah swallowed hard, hoping she would get the answer correct. "Because we believe in happy endings?"

Yesterday she would have said she did. That she believed in love again, and she had hope that it could be found, however unexpected, and that maybe this was what made it so special. But today all she could think about was how Chris had let her down, let them all down, and that it wasn't just her that was hurt. Now Hannah wouldn't have her happy ending either.

"Because we want to give our *clients* their happiest of endings," she said, but a wistful smile came over her. "And because I'd like to think that this place, this store... Well, it's my happy ending, really."

"Mine too," Sarah said, leaning forward, and this

time, she couldn't hold it in any longer. She had to tell Chloe. Now. She loved this store. Loved the bells over the door that jangled whenever it opened. Love the thrill of opening delivery boxes and seeing the most beautiful confections inside. She even loved hearing each bride's great love story, even if she might not have one of her own.

Her heart was pounding as she worked up the courage to say what had to be said. "Chloe, there's something I need to tell you."

Chloe frowned. There was no going back now.

But there was a door, with an exit. But she couldn't run. This was Hannah's wedding they were talking about. And Chloe, difficult as she could be, had given her an amazing opportunity by bringing her into Bayside Brides. She owed her this much.

"Chris Foster received an offer on Crestview. The new owner plans to take possession of the home before Hannah's wedding." She let out a breath she hadn't even realized she had been holding.

Chloe blinked at her as if trying to process this information. "So Hannah can't have her wedding at Crestview after all?"

Sarah shook her head. "Apparently not."

Chloe's eyes widened. "Wow," she eventually said. "Wow."

"I want you to know that I did everything in my power to make this happen," Sarah said, leaning into the table. "Chris...he gave me his word." Her voice cracked, damn it, and hot tears stung the back of her eyes. But she didn't even know what the tears were for. Worry? Fear? Anger? Disappointment?

She waited, her breath labored, for Chloe to say something. Anything.

Finally, Chloe tossed up her hands and said, "Well, you tried."

Sarah stared at her boss. This was not the response she had been expecting. "So...you're not mad at me?"

Chloe gave a small laugh. "Well, it's hardly your fault. Unless...is there something you're not telling me?"

"No!" Sarah sat up straighter in her chair. There was nothing she was keeping from Chloe, at least, nothing relevant. "I learned the news last night. It was very disappointing, especially because Chris and I had a deal."

Chloe frowned. "A deal?"

Right. When Chloe and Hannah had stopped by the estate sale, Chris had omitted that part, hadn't he? He'd given her credit. Undo, perhaps. Either way, it changed nothing.

"He wasted my time," she said with a sigh. "I asked him to let us hold Hannah's wedding there in exchange for me helping him to fix his house up, to help it sell. Little did I know how that would backfire on me," she added bitterly.

"You mean that you spent last week cleaning up that old mansion?" Chloe looked at her in wonder.

Sarah nodded. "I know you told me to use my time to prove that this is where I wanted to be, that this job was the right fit. I couldn't think of a better way to do that than to make sure that Hannah got the wedding she'd always wanted and that ...you didn't have to worry about it anymore. And I trusted Chris. I...believed in him."

"You opened your heart." Chloe raised her eyebrows. "Well. I have to say that I didn't expect this."

"So I can keep my job?" Sarah asked, hopefully.

"Not only can you keep your job, but I'm going to let you start helping me with my event planning projects," Chloe said. "You're passionate. You care. We have that in common. Maybe we even have another thing in common."

Sarah frowned. She could think of nothing else, other than the fact that they were both single. "What's that?"

"Maybe we care just a little too much," Chloe said with a funny smile and Sarah nodded. That much was true all right.

The blinds in the hotel room had been drawn since last night, but by morning a crack of light appeared on each side of the window. Chris supposed that there was no avoiding it. The day had come to leave Oyster Bay. Perhaps the only mistake he'd made was his own. The one thing he'd promised himself not to do, the one rule he'd set had been broken. Get in. Get out. Keep your head down.

He'd done exactly the opposite.

He'd packed his suitcase this morning, when he

couldn't lie in bed any longer, replaying the events from yesterday over and over, wondering what else he should have done, or could have done.

"I'm going to be straight with you," Jim had said when he'd appeared at Crestview, just as Chris was locking up the house. "Another buyer might not come along for months. Maybe even years."

He knew Jim was right. A house this big, bogged down by landmark status, would be a headache to most people. If they wanted waterfront property, they'd probably rather take a small condo, something they could stay in on weekends or summer vacations. A house like this was for year-round use. It needed love and attention that hadn't been given to it since Marty had moved out.

"There's no way we can push off the closing date?" he had pressed, even though Jim had made that clear. The buyers were holding firm on that. It was July. They wanted to enjoy their summer on the shore. They had a backup property in mind in a neighboring town.

The decision was obvious. He would sell to the one buyer who had come along, just as he had come here to do. He had succeeded. They had succeeded. With Sarah's help, the house looked the best it could be, better than he could have ever made it himself.

So why then, instead of feeling like he had succeeded, did he feel like he had failed?

He pulled back the blinds and stared out onto the view of the Atlantic. A premium room he'd paid extra for just so he didn't have to face town. Just so he didn't have to see people. But what he saw now was the same view he'd seen that fateful day, his last time here, shortly after that photo had been taken with Jenna.

She'd brought him to Oyster Bay to tell him the truth. That there was nothing the doctors could do. That she didn't have much time. He'd stared out onto the ocean in disbelief, his heart not wanting to believe her even though his head knew that he had to. The waves were strong that day, crashing against the shoreline in angry bursts, and he felt like they were pulling him in, taking away everything that was his, that had meant so much.

Jenna died nine weeks later. He never returned to Oyster Bay again. Not until now.

And now, he would leave it. Forever. And even though that was supposed to be his closure, and even though that was supposed to feel good, it didn't feel right.

His head knew he was making the right choice. The practical choice. After all, what was the alternative? To move into Crestview himself? To let it sit on the market, while he covered the overhead?

Impossible.

But his heart... Frankly, he hadn't even known he still had a heart. Until now. All these years, it had been numb. No pain. No joy either.

The clock on the bedside table ticked away another minute. It was check-out time, and there was no delaying the inevitable.

Chris pulled in a heavy breath as he closed the hotel room door behind him and made his way to the elevator bank, his suitcase rolling behind him. He pressed the button and stepped inside the elevator when the doors slid open, taking in the silence as he watched the buttons count down his descent to the lobby level.

Alone. He'd gotten so used to being alone for the past three years that he hadn't even realized how unhappy it had made him.

"Checking out, sir?" The woman behind the counter smiled expectantly at him as he approached. "I hope you had a pleasant stay in Oyster Bay."

He paused, feeling the impact of that simple statement, that was probably just part of the script that she was required to say to all the guests. "I did," he said, looking down at his wallet.

Once there had been a time when he couldn't recall what he'd ever found appealing about Oyster Bay. It had a dark shadow over it, despite the sunshine and sea air and brightly colored taffy being pulled in the candy shop window on Main Street.

But Sarah had lifted all that fog. Scrubbed away the dirt and the grime in that old house until she uncovered what was once so beautiful about it. She'd breathed new life into Crestview Manor.

She'd breathed new life into him.

He looked up at the woman, who seemed to be losing her patience with him as a line formed behind him.

"Sorry." He handed over the credit card, his heart pounding as she processed it and handed him his receipt.

"We hope to see you again soon," she said as her eyes slid to the person behind him.

Chris pushed his wallet back into his pocket and stared out the windows onto the street. There was no reason to ever return to Oyster Bay now. His uncle was gone. The house would be sold. His connection to this town, and everyone in it, and everything that had ever happened here, would finally be a part of his past.

Just as he had wanted it to be.

Only that wasn't what he wanted anymore at all. This town, it was a part of him, and try as he might he couldn't deny it. And leaving it all behind wouldn't just be letting Marty down. It would mean letting himself down, too.

With a sense of purpose he hadn't felt in too many years to admit, he grabbed the handle of his suitcase and crossed the lobby to the front doors, his stride quick, his chest full.

He was checking out of the hotel, but he wasn't going back to Boston. He was going three blocks down the street. To find Jim McDowell in the real estate office. Before it was too late.

Fifteen

Bayside Brides was located right in the heart of Main Street, only a short distance from the flower shop, the Oyster Bay Hotel, and The Lantern—where Chris and Sarah had never made it for their celebratory drinks.

Chris waited until a few minutes before noon to make his stop there, deciding that it was the best way to track down Sarah. The only way. He didn't know where she lived. He could, he supposed, ask around. In a town this small, the first or second person he spoke to would surely be able to guide him in the right direction, but they might also tip Sarah off, give her a reason to not be home, or not come to the door.

Truth be told, he wasn't so sure she'd want to hear him out.

He pushed inside the storefront, which was even more frilly and girly than it appeared from the outside, though it was pretty and elegant in its own, extremely feminine way. He smiled to himself, thinking of Sarah spending her days here, and what a huge shift that was from her days helping him clean up the house, with paint smeared on her cheek and dust in her hair and cobwebs lurking at every corner.

"May I help you?" A pretty brunette approached him with a curious smile. Chris imagined it wasn't every day that men came in here.

"Just browsing," he said in a low voice.

The woman's brow knitted but she smiled politely and said, "If there's anything you're, um, interested in, let me know."

He didn't know whose face was redder after that statement, and he showed her some mercy by nodding quickly and walking to the back of the store. It was a small shop, with walls of dresses and shoes and veils. A small seating area sat in front of a three-way mirror. No Sarah.

He could have asked for her. He would, and soon, if she didn't make an appearance. But he didn't want to interrupt her. He just wanted to see if she was free soon, for lunch. If she might join him.

As soon as he almost knocked down a rack of poufy bridesmaids' dresses, he knew that he had made a mistake in coming here. He would have been better off sitting outside, on a park bench, around five, waiting until she was off work for the day.

But he just couldn't wait. Each hour that went by felt like the distance between them had grown further. That soon she would slip from his reach altogether, and he couldn't have that.

He'd lost too much already. He wouldn't lose another day.

He glanced over toward the counter, catching the eye of the brunette, who quickly darted her gaze away, pretending to be extremely immersed in something on the computer screen. Right. He'd give it two more minutes and then he'd ask. Or leave. Come up with another plan, even if he was out of one at the moment.

There was no sign of Chloe, the boss. Maybe she was at a meeting.

Maybe...No, he frowned. Sarah couldn't have lost her job over the wedding venue falling through.

His heart began to pound and he was just about to step forward and ask straight up for Sarah Preston, when he saw them. The jewelry that he had given Sarah just a few short days ago. They were in the case. Tagged. For sale.

Something inside him dropped, like a heavy weight, permanently held down. There it was. All the proof he needed that Sarah had put Crestview, and everything they'd had there, behind them. That she was getting rid of the memories, the physical reminders, just as he had been determined to banish the old house.

"Excuse me?" His voice was loud, clear, surprising even to himself.

The woman looked up in something close to alarm. "Yes?"

"I am interested in something, actually." He tried to ignore the pop of her eyes as she approached. "These necklaces. This bracelet. And those earrings. I'll take them."

A funny smile crept over her mouth as she reached into her pocket and fished out a key. "Gift wrap?" she asked, with a pert little smile.

He nodded. Why not? If he was going to do something, he was going to do it right. All the way.

Something told him that Sarah wouldn't have it any other way.

He followed the woman to the counter, handed over his credit card, and waited while she rang up the order and packaged each item in a small, blue gift box. The shop was quiet, aside from the classical music that faintly filled the space. Chris trained his ear for any other sound of life. For a voice behind a white paneled door that must have led to an office of some sort. But there was nothing.

If he'd cost her her job, she'd never forgive him.

And he would never forgive himself.

"There you are," the woman said, sliding the bag across the counter to him.

He took it by the handles. Cream, thick ribbons. He opened his mouth, catching the woman's eye.

And her knowing smile. "Sarah's on her lunch break, but she should be back in about half an hour. If you want to catch her, she said she was taking her sandwich down to the beach."

He stared at the woman, wondering how she knew, but he didn't ask. He had all the information he needed. And all the encouragement, too.

And he wasn't wasting another minute.

Sarah rarely took lunch breaks, other than to dash over to Angie's for a quick sandwich, and maybe today wasn't the day to take one. Maybe today she should be back in the shop, earning her worth, proving that she belonged there, even though she knew that she did. They'd welcomed her back, and she should be happy, she should be joyous, she should feel like she'd accomplished what she'd wanted in the past week.

Instead, she felt heavier in her heart than she had before this entire mess even started.

The waves were coming in strong today, and she slipped off her shoes to venture to the waterfront. She headed north up the shoreline, thinking of Crestview in the distance, wondering if she would ever venture in that direction again, or if she could ever think back on it without a feeling of sadness.

But then, that would make her no different than Chris, wouldn't it?

She squinted into the sunshine, shielding her eyes from the glare, when she felt a tap on her shoulder. She jumped and turned, expecting to see Melanie, or maybe one of the Harper sisters—the inn wasn't too far from here and Abby was probably off work by now.

But it wasn't one of her friends.

Or maybe, she thought, as her heart began to pound in her chest, it was a friend after all.

"Chris." She stared at him, trying to make sense of

this. She'd thought he was leaving, first thing, that he couldn't wait to get out of this town, after all.

"I'm glad I found you," he said.

She shook her head. "We've said everything we needed to say. I know you're going back today." And she knew Crestview would be sold. That Hannah wouldn't be able to have her wedding there. That she'd spent the better part of a week holding up her end of the bargain to Chris.

And to Melanie, she thought. Because despite her protests, and her intention, her heart had once again won out.

But today, it was being tucked firmly back into place.

"I am going back today," he said. "But we haven't said everything there is to say. At least, I haven't."

"Chris." She closed her eyes, wanting him to go away, to leave her be, to move on, to forget about him. Because that's what people did when things hurt, wasn't it? They pushed it away, or tried to, somewhere it couldn't hurt them anymore.

She opened her eyes, looking into Chris's dark eyes, feeling her heart soften, but just a little. "I wasn't fair to you," she said.

"No, I wasn't fair to you."

"You got an offer on the house," she said with a sigh. "I couldn't expect you to turn it away, not when another buyer might not come along for years."

"I wasn't talking about the house," he said, forcing her to look at him sharply. "I'm talking about you, me, and the last few days. They were the happiest I've had in years. I didn't go looking for that. I'd turned myself off the possibility of it. I told myself I'd be happier that way. Alone. I told myself that love wasn't in the cards for me. And then I met you."

Tears prickled the back of her eyes and she stared at him, wanting to keep up the walls she'd built as much as she wanted to tear them down.

"I don't want to be stuck in the past anymore. I don't want to banish it, either. I didn't know how to find a balance, or how to move on. And then somehow...it just happened." He reached down and took her hand. It was warm and firm, and she knew that this time, he didn't intend to let go.

"I can't change my past. But I can change the future. And I want you in that future, Sarah. If you believe in happy endings and all that stuff." He grinned at her, and she narrowed her eyes ruefully, but she couldn't stay mad, much as she wanted.

"And Boston?"

"I have to go back, to settle things, but it's like you said...I can work anywhere. Why not Oyster Bay?"

Her stomach flipped with hope. "Does that mean you're keeping the house?"

He shook his head, all at once shutting down that flutter. And for some reason, the thought of that house being sold off to strangers who had no connection to it, no emotional investment in it, filled her with dread.

"A house like that is too big for one person, and I meant it when I said that I didn't want to end up like

Marty," Chris said. He squeezed her hand. "Besides, you made me think about a few things."

She looked at him suspiciously. "Go on."

"My uncle shut a lot of people out of that house. I saw how much you loved that house. I saw how much your friend loved it. It's a part of this town. It's a part of my past, but it's also a part of my history. And it's a house to be shared. So..." He waggled his eyebrows and gave her a long, deep look that went on for far too long. What was he getting at? What was he saying? What could he even suggest when it came to that house? "I talked with Jim. I've decided to donate Crestview to the town. Oyster Bay doesn't have a museum, after all, or at least, they didn't before."

She gasped, and this time the tears did start to flow. "So, it won't be sold?"

"It won't be sold. It will change. But then everything does, eventually, doesn't it?" He grinned as he reached out to brush a tear from her cheek with the pad of his thumb. "Of course, there will be a board of directors."

Her hand shot up in the air and she started to laugh.

"I had a feeling you'd be first in line. So that's a yes?"

"Yes," she said, nodding her head. "Yes."

"To the museum? Or...to us?"

"To the future," she said, dropping his hand to wrap her arms around his waist. He leaned in and kissed her, slowly, sweetly, like she had never been kissed before, like a man who was determined to prove to her that happy endings did exist after all.

Even for the nonbelievers.

Epilogue

Crestview had never looked more beautiful, and this time, Sarah knew that she was partly responsible for that, along with Chloe, of course. Together they'd worked all week long to make sure that the venue was perfect for their dear friend and client, and, with Chris's blessing, they'd even decided to hold part of the reception in the conservatory, which, along with every other inch of the estate that guests would see, had been sprinkled with Chloe's magic touch.

The gravel drive was now edged with paper lanterns, and the trees that lined the terrace had been draped with fairy lights. Flowers seemed to spill from every direction, from the garden to the centerpieces on the round tables that filled the stone patio to the rose-covered archway, under which Hannah and Dan would say their vows.

Abby had been setting up in the kitchen since yesterday and deemed the kitchen to be even more outdated than the one at Harper House, but just as functional.

Sarah poked her head through the swing door to check on her, just in case, her eyes widening when she saw the beautiful, three-tiered cake that was covered in colorful petals.

"Not edible," Abby pointed out. "But just what Hannah wanted."

"Then it's as it should be," Sarah said. "Every bride deserves one perfect day."

Abby had asked Leah to help out for the afternoon so that she could fulfill her familial duty as a bridesmaid, and she untied her apron strings now. "I suppose I'd better run and change now. The guests will be coming any minute."

A thrill of anticipation shot through Sarah, just as it did every time in the minutes leading up to the ceremony. She couldn't help it. The rush got her every time. An entire lifetime had led up until this one, beautiful moment.

She followed Abby into the hallway, where Chloe was standing with her clipboard. "I've got everything covered," she said when she spotted Sarah. "You go and enjoy yourself. You've earned it."

Sarah smiled and edged back toward the conservatory, hoping to find her date there.

"Oh, and Sarah?"

She turned, eager to see if Chloe needed anything, but her boss just gestured to her. "That jewelry looks beautiful on you."

She set a hand to her neck, where the necklace that Chris had given her rested at her collarbone. "Thank you," she said and went hurrying toward the back of the house.

Abby was right. The wedding was going to start soon. The bride was upstairs in one of the guest rooms, getting ready, and once Chloe gave her the all-clear, she would come down the stairs, and then Chloe would queue the music.

It was time to take her seat. But first, it was time to find Chris.

She found him outside on the patio, looking out onto the garden, where the chairs had been arranged to create an aisle. She hovered for a moment, wondering if he was thinking of his past, not wanting to interrupt or intrude, but he felt her stare and caught her eye. And he smiled. A smile that crinkled the corners of his eyes and made her heart fill with warmth.

"It's a beautiful place to have a wedding," he said as she came to stand beside him.

She reached down and held his hand. "I understand if you change your mind about staying."

"I don't want to turn my back on the memories anymore," he said. "Besides, we deserve a party for all the work we've put into this place."

"The music is starting," Sarah said. Guests would be filtering in soon, and then the procession would begin. "We should take our seats."

"Or we could have a dance first?"

She frowned at him. "A dance?"

"There's no one around," he said, and she had to agree with him. Yet.

"I'm a little wobbly in these heels," she said, looking down at her feet. She hadn't exactly pegged Chris for the dancing type. But then, he continued to surprise her.

He pulled her in close. "Just hold onto me."

She smiled as she leaned her head against his shoulder. That was just what she intended to do.

Keep Reading

Don't miss the final book in the Oyster Bay series!

HAD TO BE YOU

Wedding planner Chloe Larson is perfectly content helping other women find their happy endings. Love is the last thing on her mind, especially when she has a business to grow. But when a charming suitor sweeps her off her feet—literally—at a friend's wedding, she begins to see firsthand what all the hype is about.

When the opportunity to plan a high-profile wedding is presented, Chloe is thrilled to take on the task, especially when a competitive business moves into Oyster Bay...that is until she learns that the groom is Nick Tyler—the very man she has been hoping to run into again.

As plans get underway, the groom isn't the only one having doubts. Chloe has always been risk adverse, but now, she may have to take the greatest chance of all...to save her business and her heart.

About the Author

Olivia Miles is a *USA Today* bestselling author of small town romance and heartwarming women's fiction. She lives on the North Shore of Chicago with her family and an adorable pair of dogs.

Olivia loves connecting with readers. Please visit her website at www.OliviaMilesBooks.com to learn more.

*9 7 8 0 9 9 9 5 2 8 4 7 1 *